THE DARK SIDE
OF
ENLIGHTENMENT

THE DARK SIDE OF ENLIGHTENMENT

Bruce E. Weber

a Stanfield Books publication

Copyright ©2015 Bruce E. Weber

Printed in the United States of America

* * * * *

Disclaimer

This is a work of fiction. Any resemblance to actual persons, places, or events is a coincidence.

* * * * *

Cover Photo Courtesy of Bigstock.com

Formatting and Cover Design by Debora Lewis
arenapublishing.org

Editing by Harvey Stanbrough

ISBN-13: 978-1508517832
ISBN-10: 1508517835

THE DARK SIDE
OF
ENLIGHTENMENT

BRUCE E. WEBER

Contents

Christmas in Nogales

She was about 5'4" and Hispanic, and I guessed around twenty-five years old. Her skin was more café than au lait, and she had those cat-like eyes and glossy lips that drive me nuts. And her name was Ramona; I saw it on her nametag. Ramona! What a beautiful name!

Beautiful Ramona gave me a suspicious look, stepped in front of me, held up her hands and said, "We're closed, Sir... unless you're here to volunteer."

I wanted to say, *I'm here because I've been wandering the highways for years, stopping in every McDonald's along the way, looking for a girl like you, Ramona, and here, at the end of the road, at a McDonald's in Nogales Arizona on Christmas day, I've finally found you. So come on girl, let's go.* But what I said was, "I'm here to volunteer." Hey, I was telling the truth, something I almost never do.

Ramona gave me a smile. "Good! We've just heard that the first bus has crossed the border."

I asked her what she wanted me to do. She pointed to a group of people by the counter, all yakking like they were family, and told me to ask them for instructions. So I went up to the group and asked a guy with a pony tail and sandals what the deal was. He looked me over and smirked. I wanted to drag him outside and teach him not to insult people with Brooklyn accents, but then I remembered it was Christmas, and also, I didn't want Ramona to see me do such a thing.

Anyway, Ponytail mumbled that when the kids come in I should get a tray of burgers and set one in front of each kid, then ask what kind of drink they want. He looked at my shoes the whole time, like he'd never seen a pair of custom-made Italian loafers. I was straining to hear him when the school bus pulled up.

It was just a regular yellow school bus, but the top was bleached almost white by the sun. I tell you, you wouldn't believe this sun out here. I'm from back east and I'm used to working nights mostly. I don't feel real comfortable with all this light.

So anyway, a bunch of kids got out and lined up outside the store. There was this lady in a brown uniform barkin' orders at 'em in Spanish. These kids were all from across the border. This family that owns two Mc'D's in Nogales, they have this thing every Christmas. They bring busloads of kids across from Mexico and give 'em free food. I read about it in the Tucson paper and came down to help out. Even a person such as myself gets lonely on Christmas Day.

So outside, the lady in brown ushered the kids through the door, mumbling and touching each one on the shoulder. Each kid had a sheet of paper, which had something to do with immigration. They were all were skinny and wide-eyed. They came through the door lookin' scared till they saw this regulation Santa Claus the owners had hired. He looked so real I wanted to yank his beard. Soon as the kids got a look at him, their faces lit up with smiles.

When the last kid came through the door, the lady in brown didn't touch him like the others. He was a sight, this kid. He was browner than the rest and so skinny he looked like he was made of wire. His clothes were thin and ragged and way too small, but what was really strange were his shoes. The right shoe was a black high-top and way too big for him. A piece of twine knotted the top two eyeholes, and the cord had rubbed his skin raw. The left shoe was red and way too small, so tight his big toe had torn a hole in the top of it.

I didn't want him to catch me staring, so I went to work delivering burgers. I smiled and tried to make the kids feel good, but I think the food was all they needed. I worked my way around to the boy with the mismatched shoes. He was sitting with his hands folded in his lap by then, looking up at the pink and yellow pipes overhead, kicking his feet back and forth under the table. I laid two burgers in front of him and continued down the line, but I watched him from the corner of my eye. He unwrapped one, looked at it a few seconds, then took a deep bite and chewed with his eyes closed. I walked past him again and took a closer look at his face. He had a fading shiner under his left eye. A scab on his right cheek was peeling and there was raw pink skin around it.

I went back for a tray of drinks, and by the time I got back to that boy, he'd finished only half his burger. When he saw me he grabbed the other burger and put it in his lap. I asked him if he wanted a Coke or an Orange drink. He nodded a little, so I set down one of each. He looked up at me with big dark eyes and this time I couldn't look away. I can't say why. All I can say is, it was like I was lookin' in the mirror. Then somebody bumped into me and broke the spell, so I went back to delivering drinks. I glanced out the window just as two more buses pulled in.

I walked around, checking to see if everybody had what they needed. Some of the kids were wrapping their half-eaten burgers and the remains of their fries, tucking them into the bags we'd handed out. I eased over to Ramona and asked her why they were doing that, since they all looked so hungry.

"They might be saving some for their brothers and sisters, or maybe they won't have much to eat the rest of the day and don't want to finish it all now."

I was a bit hungry myself, so I asked if I could have a burger. Ramona said I could eat all I wanted, so I unwrapped one of the cheeseburgers and bit into it. But it wasn't a cheeseburger. It was some kind of dry, mealy sausage. It took all the spit I could muster to melt it down. "What is this stuff?"

"Chorizo," she said. "Mexican sausage. Cheeseburgers aren't that popular here."

Hungry as I was, I couldn't finish it.

After I stuffed it in the trash the woman in brown came back in and issued some more orders. The kids from the first bus filed out with their white paper bags. The boy with mismatched shoes stuffed his other burger under his shirt, picked up his Coke and headed out the door.

They'd cooked enough chorizo burgers to feed an army, so I took a tray-full outside. I gave three to each kid, but when I got to the boy with the odd shoes I'd run out of them. I know Spanish pretty good, 'cause I grew up around Puerto Ricans, so I told him I'd go back for more. Then I asked him his name.

He raised his chin and said, "Emilio Robles."

I got that same feeling as before, but I looked away in time. I felt like I had to do something for this kid, but I don't know why. Could'a been that goddamn sun. I think it was makin' my head soft.

Anyway, I went inside and looked behind the counter and found a big white bag. I stuffed it with chorizos and then went to an empty booth in the corner. I carry my short money in my left front pocket and my long money in my right. I peeled off a few singles and about a dozen twenties and wrapped the bills around six fifties and five hundreds. I wrapped the bills with a rubber band, tucked the rest away and stood up. Emilio was about to get on the bus so I had to hurry.

When I was walking out I was thinking how dumb this was, but what else could I do? Whoever Emilio lived with would probably rip the money, but maybe the bastards'd be decent enough get him some shoes that fit. I got to Emilio just before he reached the bus door and offered him the white sack.

He looked suspicious.

I held the roll of bills so he could see it, then stooped down and pressed the bag against him, and with the other hand I stuffed the roll of bills into his jean pocket and poked it down deep. He was startled but he didn't say anything.

I said, "Feliz Navidad, Amigo."

He wrapped his arms around the bag and squeezed. He was about to get on the bus when Ramona walked up. She smiled at him.

I stood up. "Ramona, this is Emilio Robles."

She patted Emilio on the shoulder and wished him Merry Christmas. Emilio turned and got on the bus. When I looked at Ramona, she was shaking her head and her eyes were scrunched tight. She walked away with her head bowed.

I went back for another load of burgers. I was handing them out when the bus Emilio had gotten on pulled away. I looked back to it, and saw Emilio walking toward me.

I said, "*Que pasa, hombre?*"

"Wrong bus," he said, in good English. He trotted to the end of the line. I walked along, handing out burgers and watching him from the corner of my eye. The kids were making slow progress boarding the bus because I was holding up the line. I glanced again toward Emilio. He was edging away from the back of the line. He was stepping backward with baby steps and scanning the crowd. He was easing toward the edge of the parking lot.

I doled out the burgers and wished the kids Merry Christmas in a loud voice, trying to draw attention to myself. I stole a quick look at Emilio. He was ten feet from a big brown dumpster, backing away real slow and squeezing that white bag.

The last kid in line was a little girl wearing a pink coat with a fur-lined hood. I stooped with the tray so she could stuff her pockets, and then I looked again at Emilio. He'd reached the corner of the dumpster. He looked at me, and for a couple seconds our eyes met. He was waiting to see what I'd do. I didn't move. He spun around and disappeared.

Then the bus driver hollered at the little girl. I gave him the look I give when I'm about to do something very ugly and he clammed up. The little girl's pockets were full, but there were four burgers left, so I stuffed them in the hood of her coat. When she stepped up, the driver grabbed the lever and slammed the door.

I walked back into the store and picked up a tray of drinks. Then the door flew open. The woman in brown rushed in and almost rammed me. She looked around the store and shouted, "Emilio Robles! Emilio Robles, are you here?"

She spoke to Mister Ponytail, but he shook his head. Then she walked up to me. "Have you seen a little boy wearing a black T-shirt, with a scab on his face? I can't find him. We do not have his immigration slip."

Before I could say anything, Ramona spoke up. "He left on bus 406. I saw him get on."

"Are you sure it was him?"

She shrugged. "Who could forget such a boy?"

The woman looked at me.

"I saw him get on bus 406," I said. Hey, it was the goddam truth!

Brown-shirt walked away shaking her head. I turned to Ramona, feeling a strong need to engage her in conversation, but she went back to serving food.

I tried to stay busy, but I couldn't stop thinking about Emilio. I was having bad visions of what could happen to him in a place like Nogales. What if he was grabbed by some molester? Or joined a street gang? Now I felt like a fool. I thought I was helping the kid, letting him get away. What I'd done was let him escape into a world that would eat him alive.

Another bus had come in, and after the kids were all served, I got this urge to talk to Ramona, to fess up about what I'd done. When I looked over at her, she was wiping tables. She smiled and waved, but my worries about Emilio were nagging at me. I waved back and headed out to my car.

The sky had turned cloudy and the wind was raw. It was beginning to feel a lot more like Christmas. I spent the next two hours combing the streets and alleys of downtown Nogales, asking myself what I'd do when I found Emilio Robles. At first I didn't know, and then I knew exactly what I'd do. I'd go back to that McDonalds and I'd take Ramona aside and I'd tell her that if she hooked up with me permanently, I'd turn myself into the best man she ever knew and she'd never want for anything the rest of her life. She could quit her job and spend her time bossing servants and taking care of little Emilio and buying him all the shoes he wanted. You might not think she'd go along with that, but I knew she would because... well, let's just say I can be a very persuasive person.

But I couldn't find him. It got dark and the Christmas lights came on, and finally I gave up. I sat at a stoplight through six light changes, thinking how lucky I was that I didn't find that kid and hook up with Ramona. Me, a husband? I was a woman's worst nightmare. And me, a father? I wasn't fit to raise cockroaches.

I was ready to head home, but before I left, I had to go by McDonald's for one last look at beautiful Ramona. I knew it was stupid but I couldn't stop myself. I came toward the restaurant from the north, through an alley lined with a barbed-wire fence. Out of the corner of my eye, I saw a yellow sandwich wrapper skip by in the wind, and a few feet ahead, I stopped. I looked to my left. In a narrow space between two wooden shacks, Emilio Robles was sitting in a pile of wadded wrappers. He stood up when he saw me. He had that crumbled McDonald's bag in his left hand, and his little belly stuck out like he'd swallowed a basketball. He walked toward me with his skinny right arm outstretched, offering me his last chorizo burger.

The Confluence

All you could hear was the river. It made that soft rustling sound, like leaves blown across pavement, the sound water makes when it's in a hurry.

I was sitting on the wooden balcony of a rustic motel in Idaho, looking down on the Salmon River. Its waters were Coke-bottle pale at the edges, but toward the middle they darkened to a deep jade green. The surface was mottled with froth because the Salmon's an eager river. It yearns to merge with other rivers and, after gathering forces with them, to meld into the blue Pacific.

I leaned back in a plastic lawn chair, resting from a backpacking trip on the river. After ten days in the woods, I had decided to sleep in a soft bed for a night before taking the long drive home. I watched the river pass from left to right until it swirled with the incoming flow of its North Fork, which joins the main river about thirty yards downstream from where I was sitting.

The sound of the river soothed me like a lullaby, and after I'd showered and shaved and planted myself in that plastic chair, all I needed was a couple cold beers and I'd be ready for that king-sized bed. But it was mid-afternoon, too soon to give up on the day. Though my head kept nodding onto my chest, I didn't want to go napping and leave such a comforting scene, so I pulled myself awake, thinking I'd get some coffee. I rubbed my eyes and looked downstream. A fly-fisherman was at the inside corner of the spot where the North Fork joins the main river at a right angle, and he was working his line across the water, his back toward me. He lifted his arm and drew the line behind him, then swung down to throw it onto the swirling surface. The rhythmic movements were almost hypnotic. I shook my head and blinked, fighting the pull of sleep.

I looked to my left. Two young girls were tossing a beach ball. The taller one, red-haired, overfed, and maybe twelve years old, overthrew her toss to the thin blond-haired one, who was a little younger and shorter. The skinny one leaped for the ball, but it floated over her fingers and settled onto the river.

The ball floated along near the water's edge. The girls ran beside it, hoping to grab it, but the current pulled it away from shore. The girls huddled. The red-haired girl said, "Mom'll be mad." Then the little blond said, "I'm gonna get it." She turned and ran toward a silver motor home in the parking lot. The red-haired girl hesitated for a moment, then followed. I envisioned the little blond telling her mother about the ball and catching hell for carelessness. That's what I thought she meant when she said she'd "get it," but I was wrong.

The beach ball passed my balcony, and as I watched it drift, I remembered that the Salmon had been named the River of No Return by Lewis and Clark. But the ball was stalled on its journey to the Pacific. It began to orbit within the vortex created by the meeting of the waters. The swirling water contained the ball in a clockwise holding pattern about fifteen feet from shore.

I heard footsteps on the gravel. The blond girl was trotting by, wearing a pink two-piece swimsuit and trailing a yellow beach towel, followed by the red-haired girl. The redhead shouted, "Becky, don't do it!"

Becky ran along the bank, heading for the spot where the ball was trapped, and when my foggy brain caught on to her plan, a sting of panic raced through my rib cage. I'd swam in that river the day before, and though it was mid-August, the current was much too swift and the water much too cold for a bony little waif like Becky. I lurched forward from the chair and looked down the bank, hoping to see the fly-fisherman, but he was gone.

Becky arrived at the confluence. She was on the bank, looking at the ball, poised, leaning forward. The red-haired girl caught up with her. I couldn't hear what she was saying, but by her actions she was imploring Becky to stay out of the river. Becky turned and looked at her friend, then dropped the towel. She looked again at the red ball. It was held fast in the whirlpool, circling its edge, beckoning.

There wasn't time to go through the room and down the front steps. If Becky went into that maelstrom, I'd have to go over the rail. My feet were bare and I'd be landing on rough gravel, but If I hung from the deck and dropped, I doubted I'd break any bones.

I stood at the rail, my attention glued to Becky. She was through pondering. She kicked off her rubber sandals and tiptoed into the water. The bank and river bottom were littered with slippery stones, a real challenge to bare feet. Becky eased down over them, never hesitating until she was chest-deep in the river. I had my left leg over the railing, watching. She took one more step and the river swallowed her. The red-haired girl screamed.

My left foot slipped off the edge of the deck and I dropped, but I caught myself by the crook of my right leg. I was holding the top of the rail, but as I slid my right leg over, the fabric of my jeans caught on a railing nail. If I didn't get straightened up, I'd drop on my side and surely break something, and I'd be of no use in helping Becky. I was struggling to get my leg free when I glanced toward the river.

Becky was gone, I was sure of it. Still struggling to get my leg free, I glanced again toward the river. That beach ball burst from the water like it was shot out of a cannon and sailed toward the river bank.

Then Becky shot up from the dark green surface. She bobbed once, put her head back, and spit out a long, streaming arc of river water. She settled back in the water and shook her head, sending a whirl of drops from her long ponytail. I clung to the rail, watching her. Her strokes were long and smooth, and despite the strong current, she got to the shore with ease.

I was startled when, right below me, a woman screamed, "Becky!" Her voice carried more anger than fear. She passed below me, running barefoot on the jagged gravel. She was red-haired, dressed in blue jean coveralls, and she ran with her hands pressed to the sides of her head.

I was working hard to get back on the balcony, but I couldn't keep my eyes off Becky. She was standing beside the river, shivering, huddled in her own arms, while her friend held the beach ball. When the woman reached the girls, she took the ball from the red-haired girl and pointed at Becky, shaking one finger like she was hitting the kid with a stick. I couldn't make out the words, but it was a lecture, no doubt about that. Becky bowed her head and took the scolding in silence.

I was finally able to pull myself back over the rail. When I had both feet back on the deck, a wave of relief passed over me. I was rubbing my sore hands and trying to regain my composure, my gaze still on the trio as they came toward my balcony.

The woman had Becky by the arm. Her finger was still wagging up and down, stopping momentarily at the bottom of each stroke as she drove a point home. "What if your mother heard about this? If I knew you did things like this, I never would have brought you with us." The red-haired girl followed, tossing the red ball high and letting it bounce. As they passed beneath me, I felt obliged to honor the display of grit I'd witnessed. I looked down and said, "Hey swimmer."

All three looked up, startled to find they'd been observed. The mother's face was ashen. The red-haired girl's was ruddy. Becky's pale blue eyes widened like she'd heard a voice from the sky. I said, "Good job, girl."

Her shivering blue lips spread wide in a gap-toothed smile. She didn't reply, but as they walked on she jerked her arm from the woman's grasp, turned to look up at me, and waved. I watched her pass, and I kept my eyes on Becky until the three disappeared around the corner. The last one to pass from view was the red-haired girl, still tossing the beach ball skyward.

I was still looking in their direction, still absorbing the little drama, when a few seconds later that ball came bouncing happily downhill, as if drawn by an inexorable magnetism, back down into the river.

Father Juniper

On a high ridge in the Catalina Mountains of southern Arizona, beside a primeval game trail, stands a gnarled, weather-worn juniper tree. In defiance of limb-snapping cold and desert heat, it has endured for over ten centuries, outliving all other members of its species on the mountainside. A silent witness to the movements of generations of Apache Indians, it might even have overseen the confused wanderings of Francisco Coronado and his men.

None of these facts would have impressed Burt Foster. To him, it was just a big tree. He was on a hike to escape from his office, but he hadn't escaped it—he'd only left it physically—and as he climbed the trail approaching the old tree, the noise in his mind was as loud as the racket in his workplace.

His shirt was soaked with sweat when he reached the tree, so he sat on a boulder, took off his knapsack, and looked up at the towering branches. The crown was thick with blue-green needles. The immense branches spread wide, ending in thick, fingerlike points. The blackened bark that remained was checked into small squares, but most of the tree was bare, silvery wood that had been burnished smooth by the wind. The trunk was wider than the span of Burt's arms, anchored by massive roots that buckled the ground and uplifted bounders. He scanned the tree from bottom to top again, and when he reached the top, he said in a respectful whisper, "You are one big, old tree."

His butt ached from sitting on the boulder, so he sat on the ground at the base of the tree. He was cooling down fast in the steady breeze and his shirt had gone cold, so he leaned back against the tree. He tried to think of something more appropriate to his surroundings, but quotas, accounts, and customer complaints were roiling in his brain, turning his stomach into a burning core.

He sat up, unable to relax. The thoughts came faster, even as he tried to quell them. Every idea gave rise to a new problem, and every solution gave birth to another complication. If he settled an employee dispute, the solution might cause jealousy in another division. If he worked out a way to satisfy a customer, it might lead to a policy change and send costs through the roof.

He strained to breathe deep, forcing himself to draw in the cool air, but he felt like his chest was being squeezed. He shivered, then eased back into the curve of the tree trunk. That helped a little. The drumming of his heart slowed. He focused on a blue jay as it pecked the rocky ground.

The wind shifted and the sun dimmed behind a bank of clouds moving up from the south. The scent of a sweet new moisture was building in the air, and he thought he should get back to his car. *If it storms in these high parts, I could get struck by lightning, and—and what? What if I do get struck by lightning, sitting under this tree, high in these mountains? It'd be days before they'd find my body.* It was Friday, and since he'd cancelled his weekend hookups with friends, nobody would miss him until Monday. The critters would have their way with his corpse, and whoever found him would be in for a hell of a shock.

He chuckled at the thought. He'd always imagined a more dramatic death for himself, something heroic, like getting killed saving a busload of school kids, or rescuing a woman from gang rape. But all it would take was one jolt from the sky, and he'd be a crispy snack for the wildlife. He waited for a response to rise from his mind, a joke or a barb or a cynical comment about the perils of the wilderness, but nothing came. He seemed to have no response to the notion of his death.

His back and neck muscles softened and began to glow with warmth. The glow spread down his body. He looked at his feet, at the worn, dusty hiking boots. His toes had gone toasty, the muscles of his legs had eased, and all the tightness from his uphill hike had faded.

Then he felt something odd in his lower back, or rather the odd absence of something. That part of his spine no longer ached. He'd had a chronic backache since his high school football years, a mysterious, stabbing pain that tortured his waking hours and often cost him sleep. He'd long ago accepted it as part of the landscape of his life, but now the incessant pain was gone. His clenched vertebrae had slackened and melted into the gentle curve of the tree. The muscles of his shoulders let go, and he lay his head to one side. His breathing eased. The cool breeze rolled over his cheeks and forehead. There was no sound but the wind in the trees. The clamor in his head had stopped.

All the chronic annoyances of his life, the naggings that symbolized living, had come to a halt. For a moment, he thought he might be dying. He had a vague sense that if he didn't get up, his vital force would seep away and he'd be found with his eyes pecked out by some relentless blue jay.

Despite those morbid thoughts, he had neither the will nor even the desire to move. For a moment he feared he couldn't move if he wanted to. He wiggled his toes. Then he realized he was choosing to sit, awaiting a thunderbolt that could shock him dead.

The air grew heavier, charged with the energy sweeping up from the south. The wind hissed through the needles of the old juniper. The clouds blackened, tumbling lower as they rolled by. A shot of lightning cracked the sky, followed by a series of streaks, moving closer up the mountain. Fat drops splattered on the pink granite boulders, but Burt didn't move. A calming thought came to him: *If I am to die here and now, in this state of rapturous peace, so be it*.

The rain came softly at first, then in heavy waves, occasionally ripped by more lightning. The air vibrated with thunder after each flash, and then the wind picked up again. Though it was mid-afternoon, the sky was darker than dusk.

The rain fell for almost an hour, and then a band of light spread low in the eastern sky. The storm was moving away. Despite the downpour, only a few drops of rain had splattered on his jeans. A blast of lightning struck within a hundred feet, shaking the ground. The shock stung his eardrums but his body didn't stiffen. He breathed the electric air in long, slow drafts, feeling as if something malignant was seeping away from him every time he exhaled.

As he watched the storm fade, an occasional thought would start to form, then quietly pass as if the power had been shut off. The silence in his mind kept him from moving. If he moved from the tree, the noise might begin again, and he never wanted to end the stillness that had overtaken him.

But eventually he did move, obeying a primal urge to be mobile again. He felt an immediate chill when he separated from the tree, the same cold he felt when he was alone at night and couldn't sleep.

He stood up and extended his hands to the tree. He held them inches away at first, afraid of what might happen if he made contact. But he knew what would happen. He leaned forward, and the instant he touched the tree, the cold left him.

He jerked his hands away and stepped back, then looked up at the treetop. Drops of rainwater fell from its branches onto his face. He closed his eyes and reopened them, wiped the water from his eyes, then picked up his bag and headed up the trail.

The merciful stillness in his mind lasted until the following Tuesday, when an angry phone call from his district manager in Boston brought back the familiar clamor. By Thursday night Burt knew he had to go back up the mountain to sit under that old tree. His visits to the mountain became a weekly ritual. As the months passed, his quiet state of mind lasted longer into the week, but never past Thursday night. He tried once to miss a week at the tree, but by ten o'clock that Friday morning he knew it was hopeless. He left his office in Tucson without a word of explanation. He was tired of lying to his staff about his whereabouts on Fridays, and he refused to tell anyone he was having a serious personal relationship with a tree.

He'd given the old tree a name: Father Juniper. He didn't regard the tree as paternal, but priestly. He also had no particular use for spiritual matters, but he knew the name was appropriate.

He had to go to Boston for a meeting, and the Friday before he left he caught himself saying goodbye to Father Juniper. He was speaking to the tree, telling it things he told nobody else, and he wasn't a bit disturbed by the fact that the whole silly business felt natural and right. He sat at the base of the tree, conversing with it as if it were an old friend, until almost dark. If the moon had been full, he'd have stayed longer.

On his last morning in Boston, he heard on the TV news of a fire sweeping across the Catalinas. The newscast showed the flames licking up the northern face of the range. A careless camper had set fire to one of the eastern passes, and the winds were carrying the fire up the valleys, toward the peak where Father Juniper was waiting.

Burt was distracted all that day. He read more about the fire in the newspapers as he rode home on the plane. Fifty miles from Tucson, the smell of the fire drifted into the airplane, and the northern sky was smudged with the oily black smoke of burning pines.

It took a week to contain the fire, and another week before the road up the mountain reopened. Burt was in line with dozens of sightseers as they crept up the mountain highway. When he parked at the trailhead there were no other cars, since entry to the burned area was prohibited. He ignored the *Stay*

Out signs, ducked under the yellow tape, and hurried up the trail.

He passed stands of blackened timber that rose from charred soil through an atmosphere heavy with the smell of burnt wood. There were no signs of life, no birds or squirrels, no wind to carry away the smell of death. He stumbled over piles of blackened treefall, once falling so hard on his knee that he had to sit and wait for the pain to subside, but as soon as he could he limped up the trail, breathing heavily in the thin air

He stopped before rounding the final bend in the trail and asked himself whether it might be better not to know, to take his happy memories of the great tree and go back down the mountain. Then he could remember the old juniper in all its glory, not as a burnt relic. But he took a tentative step, then another, then another, and as he rounded the bend he caught his breath. *I should have stayed away....*

The canopy of surrounding forest was gone. Sunlight glared on the once-shady area and reflected from the mineralized soil. There were still some green needles left on Father Juniper's branches, but what had been the wind-burnished gray of his lower trunk was scorched and shiny black. Burt moved forward as if approaching the body of a dear friend in a mortuary, needing to verify the loss but dreading the sight. There was no breeze and the birds were gone, leaving an eerie silence.

He stood at the spot where he had sat so many times. He recalled the time he had first held out his hands, afraid to touch the tree. He was afraid again now, because he'd be able to feel whether the tree was still alive.

Then he remembered that the old tree had withstood many fires and had always come back, had always sprouted new needles and branches, and he felt a surge of hope. He reached both hands to within an inch of the blackened bark, paused for a moment, then leaned forward. He knew the truth in an instant. The great tree was not dead, but the proud old giant was dying. He leaned gently against the tree and pressed his cheek to it, but he was surprised to find that he felt no sadness, no sense of loss. Instead, he had the odd sensation that his skin was stretching, as if it were too small to contain his flesh.

A wordless thought came to him, and he knew its truth with his whole being: the old tree was passing on, but only the wood was dying. Without understanding or needing to understand, he embraced the tree, leaning against it. The feeling was inexplicable. His body tingled at every point of contact.

Gradually, the baffling sense of magnetism eased. He backed away slowly and sat on the big boulder where he'd sat during his first visit. He replayed that scene in his mind, then recounted every visit. The familiar stillness spread through him again, seeping, seemingly, into his cells, into his soul.

The afternoon gave way to dusk. He had no flashlight, so he knew he had get back to the road. He searched his mind for parting words to be said over a dead friend, but realized that no words were necessary. He looked out over the valley and felt a sudden revulsion at the sight. He never wanted to see it again.

As he thought to move up the trail, he had trouble lifting his feet. They seemed almost grown to the ground, and he advanced in shuffling, jerking steps, as if he'd topple over if he tried to move faster. He moved steadily, and fifty yards up the trail he began to sense a new lightness, a fresh energy, as if walking were a newfound pleasure, as if movement was an end in itself. His gait quickened smoothly and his stride lengthened. When he reached his car after the long trek back, he felt no fatigue, only an irrepressible urge to be always moving.

As he drove down the mountainside, every bend in the road seemed fresh and new. The sensation of speed was intoxicating. He felt obsessed with the urge for motion. His toes squirmed in his boots and his sweaty palms squeezed the leather-covered steering wheel. He lowered the windows and relished the feeling of wind on his face. Though he had seen them countless times before, he was mesmerized by the changing scenes as he wound down to the desert below.

When he reached the base of the mountain, he knew he wouldn't remain for long in the city where he'd lived his life or at the job he'd long despised. His future was laid out before him as if on a map. He would never stop moving, and he would forever crave the next horizon, almost as if he'd been freed at long last from centuries rooted in one spot.

One Night on LaGrange Street

The first things I noticed were the deep gouge in the door jamb and the wood splinters scattered on the ground. The damage had been done with a heavy crowbar, jammed in and pushed, and whoever'd done it wasn't worried about being seen or heard.

I was on the porch of a bungalow on Sloan Avenue, investigating a break-in. The house had the same peeling paint and dirty windows as its neighbors, and you'd think no burglar would waste time with it. This house was also in a neighborhood called Stringtown, where nobody had anything worth stealing, but sometimes I forget that junk is valuable stuff to people who have nothing.

From behind the door came the sound of a TV sitcom, one with a laugh track. I listened for a few seconds and then knocked. A shadow passed over the peephole glass, and when the porch light came on I stepped back so I could be seen clearly.

"What do you want?" a woman said.

"I'm Officer Lewis, Ma'am. It's about the break-in."

She asked me to hold up my badge so she could see it. I did. Then a deadbolt slid and the door pulled back slightly, still chained. She looked me up and down, then let the chain off and eased the door open.

I stepped inside. The room was lit by a small portable TV. The sitcom was in black and white, and its light, filtered through heavy clouds of cigarette smoke, filled the room with a blue haze. The place had that brackish, tinny smell, like the stale air of a bar at 3 a.m.

The woman sat down on a sagging red couch and stubbed her cigarette in a green glass ashtray that was overflowing with butts. "Sit down," she said.

Her name was Doris Palmer, age 42, but she looked older. Her bleached hair was losing to the persistent grey, and her smeared makeup couldn't hide the sags and wrinkles, but what aged her most was the scared look in her eyes.

I sat on the other end of the couch and took out my notepad. "I wonder if maybe you could tell me the approximate time of—"

She shook her head and waved her hand. "I know who it was. I can tell you who did it."

I waited for her to say more. She didn't, so I said, "How do you know?"

She shook her head and lit another cigarette, her hand trembling as she raised the lighter. She kept looking at the television. I thought it was best to give her time. She had to get used to me. She sucked on the cigarette, then spoke with the smoke streaming out of her lips. "How long have you been a cop?"

"Twenty-one years."

"You remember those three guys they found dead over on LaGrange Street back in '92?"

I was so stunned by her question that I didn't answer right away, but there was no way I could forget that business. Finally I nodded. "I remember the case. How does it relate to this break-in?"

She flipped the ash from her cigarette. It tumbled down the pile of butts and shattered on the tabletop. "Ever hear of a man named Dale Norton?"

I pretended I hadn't.

"He's out to get me. He's afraid I'll talk, now that Boyd has told his story."

I knew Dale Norton from another situation, when I'd had to restrain him to keep him from stomping a teenage kid who'd insulted him. But I didn't know anything about this Boyd character.

"Who's Boyd?"

"He's a guy in prison, down in Florida. He got hooked on some religion thing and confessed to his part in them murders, the ones on LaGrange. Dale's gotta know about it, 'cause it was in the papers. Now he's after me to shut me up. See, I'm the only other person who knows... besides Boyd, I mean. I was there. I saw it all."

I sat dead still. I didn't want to say anything that could break the spell. If this lady was for real, I was about to get an eyewitness account of one of the biggest mysteries that had ever beset this city. Back in November of 1992, three big, strong guys, all in their early thirties, were found in various rooms of a rental house on LaGrange Street. Their hands were tied behind their backs, and their throats were slit from ear to ear.

The LaGrange Street murders had never been solved. Trails led in several directions, but ended nowhere. There were rumors about mob connections, since it was such an efficient and bloody hit. There were allegations about a crooked real estate deal involving a downtown property that was earmarked for a new Sports Arena. The dead guys had been partners in a business that stored company records on computer discs, and there was some suspicion they'd copied something that had gotten them killed. There was speculation about gambling debts, and then there was a convoluted theory that they were blackmailing a high-placed official who got fed up and hired outside experts to shut them up.

One theory got almost no attention. Each of the victims had a notebook filled with the names of local females. It appeared they were having a contest to see who could have sex with the most women in a calendar year. Since the murders occurred in November, the books were pretty full. Several husbands got visits from the police and a few marriages went down the tubes, but then the issue was dropped. There were a few other theories, but no suspects, and as I waited for the woman to compose herself, I wondered what good it would do to dredge up the whole mess again.

She asked me if I wanted a drink and I declined. She left the room and came back with a bottle and a couple glasses. She poured vodka into one and held the glass with both hands, working up her nerve.

I wanted a glass of that stuff myself. Drops of cold sweat were easing down my ribs, my throat had gone dry and the smoke from her cigarette was burning my eyes, but all I could do was wait.

She took a long drink and a deep breath. Then the words came out in a low hiss, like steam being released from a boiler. "There was blood everywhere, all over the floor, on the walls, even up on the ceiling."

My toes curled, like they did when I was on top of a Ferris wheel.

"Robert was the first one. He was the only one Dale really wanted. They had him kneel on the floor. Boyd was holding the shotgun. Then Dale... Dale took hold of Robert's hair and pulled his head back. He had a straight-razor. He used it real slow."

She was trembling, staring at the TV but not seeing it. Then her eyes bulged. "The blood went everywhere and this awful gurgling sound came out. Then he... he just dropped."

I was beginning to get that feeling in the middle of my ribcage, the one I'd had only a few times in all my years on the police force. And I was hurting to get out of that room, to get some clean air in my lungs, but I wanted to hear every word Doris had to say.

"Then we heard somebody come to the door. It was Lenny, coming home. Boyd got behind the door. When Lenny came in, Boyd stuck the gun in his back and they took him to the other bedroom. We went in, and they did the same to him. He never said a word, Lenny didn't. His eyes were real wide, like... like he didn't quite believe it was real. He looked at me just before Dale—"

She was getting pretty wobbly. Her skin was shiny and pale and a bead of sweat was glistening on her upper lip. She was clenching that glass of vodka so hard her knuckles were white. She was reliving the whole thing, and it was as real to her as the night it had happened. "We were leaving when Earl showed up. They pushed him down right there in the living room. He kept saying, 'Please don't kill me! I didn't do nothin'!' He looked at me the same way Lenny had, like I could do something to help him. Some of his blood got on me."

She squeezed the glass in both hands and began shaking her head almost uncontrollably, like she was saying no to the whole thing. Then she started to shiver. She made some funny noises I couldn't make out, and then she looked right at me, as if she'd just noticed I was there. "Then Dale, he started laughing. I'll never forget that laugh. Then he said, 'That'll teach 'em to mess with my woman.' But he wasn't finished. He made me go in the bedroom where they'd killed Lenny. There was a typewriter in there."

When she mentioned the typewriter I knew she was telling the truth because that was the only detail about the crime that had never been made public. Everyone had ignored it at the time.

"He told me to type something about this being what happened to anyone who messed with his woman. But I only got a couple words typed before he stopped me. He knew it was a stupid thing to do. Then we heard a noise outside and we got out."

I waited a long moment to let her relax a bit. "So... how did Dale find out about you and Robert? Did he know about the contest these guys had going?"

She nodded. "He was in a bar one night. He heard the boys bragging about their scores. It was right after Dale and me had a fight, and I'd been with Robert a few times. Dale heard Robert say something about me being a great f—" She was shivering so badly that she choked on the last word. She closed her eyes and raised her hands to cover her face, muffling her voice somewhat. "The blood... Oh God, the blood!"

I knew she was right, I mean, about all the blood, because I had been there and seen it with my own eyes. I looked over at the TV, and through the blurred images on the screen I went back twenty years, back to LaGrange Street on that cold Friday night in November. The paper boy had called the police. He'd come to collect for the weekly paper and looked in the window. The bodies were still warm when I got there, and I'd stepped in some of that blood myself. It was like stepping in grease, and the coppery smell made my stomach roll.

That's why I had that same old feeling as I listened to Doris, that sick feeling every human being gets when he suddenly realizes in his gut that death is real. I was a young hard-ass at the time, and that night on LaGrange Street was the first time I'd ever felt it.

I'd radioed for help, and in a half-hour the place was overrun with police from Homicide and from Vice, slipping around in the blood and gawking at the mess. I lingered for a few minutes, watching one standard police procedure after another being broken. Then the chief showed up and restored some order to the proceedings. That's when I left and went back to my sector. I spent the rest of that shift nursing a pint bottle of Smirnov and wishing I'd followed my uncle's advice to be a plumber.

The sound of Doris sobbing and moaning brought me back to the present. But the sweat I had on me now was as cold as the one I'd had that night on LaGrange Street, and I had the feeling that no time at all had passed since that bloody Friday night. Anyway, I got busy writing down the details of what she'd told me. When I got to the part about Robert's boast in the bar, I remembered what had happened after the murders.

A whole can of worms was opened. The investigation into the murders led to suspicions of police corruption. There were allegations of intentional mishandling of evidence, and that led to a federal investigation involving the city and county police, a mob boss named Norman Glick, and a widespread fencing operation involving stolen TV sets. The mess lingered for years. Ten policemen lost their jobs and two were indicted. One committed suicide.

But we never solved the case. It was reopened from time to time, and there'd been more speculation, but never any arrests. Then a couple years ago the press had reported that most of the material evidence from the crime had been lost. The official line was that it had been misplaced during a move to the new headquarters. There were unkind words in the newspapers about the police department, but it all died down. I was lost in these memories when Dolores laid her cold hand on mine.

"I never told anybody about it," she said. "The police questioned me. I wanted to tell them, but I knew Dale'd get me if I did. Now that Boyd's talked, though, Dale has to shut me up. He knows nobody'll believe Boyd unless I talk."

I put my hand over hers and squeezed. Then I called my chief and told him the story. He'd been a detective at the time and remembered all the details. When I mentioned the typewriter, he knew Doris was for real.

The chief told me someone from Homicide would be there soon to take over, and I left shortly after that. Doris got 24-hour police protection from then on. The case was reopened, and it was about to go to the Grand Jury when somebody in that Florida prison put a knife in Boyd Driscoll's ribs. That left Dolores as the only witness, but she was so flaky that the prosecutor didn't think he could make a case based on her testimony alone. So the whole thing disappeared again.

They took the police protection off Doris a short time later. Dale Norton had been admitted to the hospital, suffering from colon cancer. It took nine months for the disease to sap his life away, so I guess some kind of justice was done, even though fate delivered it.

Speaking of justice, that famous statue of Justice always shows her blindfolded, but in the case of the LaGrange Street murders, it was us cops who were blind. We'd convinced ourselves the crime was part of some elaborate scheme. Nobody wanted to believe it was just a petty domestic squabble, brought on by a careless boast overheard in a bar.

I remember thinking when I left Doris's place that the human race would be a lot better off if it could just keep its mouth shut. But then, if it weren't for informants, we wouldn't solve too many crimes, so I guess it all evens out.

AN OLD ZIPPO

The champagne was vintage and properly chilled. The three dozen red roses were poised to open, spreading their perfume through the wide, high-ceilinged living room. A generous mound of pearly-black Beluga caviar nestled in a bowl of crushed ice, and a soft Brazilian love song, cooed by a sultry female voice, drifted from well-placed hidden speakers. A trio of silver candelabras bathed the area in a soft glow.

After opening a long expanse of drapes to let in the last rays of twilight, the creator of this seductive scene stood back to observe it. He decided it was as perfect as he could make it, so he walked to his bedroom to apply the final details.

He buttoned his black silk shirt and tucked it into his black pleated trousers. He slipped his feet into cap-toed oxfords, bent to tie the thin laces, then stood before the full-length mirror. He was pleased with what he saw, but he had no illusions. No matter how austerely trim, smoothly tanned and muscular a 52 year-old man was, nothing could obscure the fact that he had reached the brink of geezer-hood, and he wondered how good he could possibly look to the 28 year-old woman who'd soon appear at his door.

He ran a comb through his thick, dark hair and headed for the kitchen. Before he opened the fridge, he looked at the calendar sheet that was taped to its door. He'd marked off each day of the month until this one, and within its square he'd printed *Carmen leaves*. Next to it was her 5 x 7 photo. He pulled it off and looked at it.

She was looking away from the camera, but both her large, dark eyes were visible. She was obviously Hispanic, though her complexion was light and her long hair was tawny. Her nose was irregular, broken during early childhood, and its slight hump gave her face a hint of American Indian blood. The full lips of her wide mouth were parted in a smile.

He dropped the picture into a drawer and tried to shake himself from the fog that overtook him whenever he thought of her. He glanced at his watch. She was late, but he'd expected that. He was crumpling the calendar sheet when the doorbell rang.

At the entry, he checked his shirttail and smoothed back his hair. When he opened the door, the influx of air brought a heavy mist of perfume, thick with flowers and spice. His gaze met Carmen's, held it through her smile, then drifted down her body. She was wearing a black satin dress, embarrassingly low-cut, its hem a foot above her knees.

"Hello," Henry said, his throat suddenly tight.

"Hi, Henry."

He stood aside to let her pass. "Our reservation is for 9:00, so we've got time for a drink and a little snack." Carmen slid past him, her perfume intensifying at close range. Henry knew the scent, but couldn't name it.

"Oh, I love your place," she said. "It's so airy and spacious. And that seascape painting... it's breathtaking."

"It's a scene from someplace in Mexico, I think. Please sit down; I'll be right back."

Carmen sat on the sofa and gazed around the room. Henry went to the sideboard and returned with a silver ice bucket and a long, thin tray.

"Oh my God!" Carmen said. "How'd you know Taittinger is my favorite?"

"Intuition, I guess." Henry looked into her eyes, straining to keep his attention from dropping to her cleavage. He opened the bottle and filled the glasses. "Here's to your success in Portland, Carmen. I do hate to see you go."

"Thanks. I'm really excited about it." She took a sip from the slender glass. "But ever since we met, I've felt some doubts about leaving."

Henry's hand trembled slightly when he set down his glass. He spread caviar on a wedge of thinly sliced toast and handed it to Carmen, but she didn't take it. She leaned forward and opened her mouth, and he slid it onto her tongue.

"Ummm, that's nice," she said.

Henry topped off their glasses. They sat for a half-hour, sipping and chatting and laughing; they always seemed to laugh hysterically at things no one else found the least bit funny. As the final light of dusk faded and the room darkened, Henry poured the third refill.

Carmen said, "You don't smoke, do you?"

"No, do you?"

"No, I just wondered about this." She picked up a battered Zippo lighter from the tabletop. She looked at the inscription engraved on it. "What's 'Fender' mean?"

"It's a brand of guitar. There's a kid named Ricky who makes deliveries to our office. I think he comes to your office too. Anyway, he gave it to me."

"I know him. He's a cute little guy and he's really funny."

"He's been on his own since he was 16. Kid had never even seen a dentist. He told me one day he had a bad toothache, so I took him to my dentist. Last week she finished up on him, and I gave him a ride home. When I dropped him off, you know what he said?"

She tilted her head, ready for the answer.

"He said, 'Thanks, for caring.' I almost started bawling on the way home."

"How sweet," Carmen said, raising her lipstick-smeared glass to her lips.

"So the next day, he gave me this lighter. He's a guitar player and a smoker, so I bet that Zippo's one of his prize possessions. I bet it's thirty years old. I gave him my phone number and told him to call me if he ever needs help."

He took the lighter from her, clicked the lid open and shut, then laid it on the glass tabletop. When he looked up, she was staring into his eyes. *Now*, he thought. He leaned closer and kissed her. The heaviness of her perfume filled his lungs. Her lips were so soft he had to fight the urge to bite them. He reached one hand to her shoulder and the strap of her dress fell down her arm.

Carmen didn't resist. She sighed.

He was about to make his next move when the phone rang. He'd forgotten to shut off the ringer. After six rings, the answering machine kicked on. As Henry slid the other strap down Carmen's arm, a voice came on the recorder.

"Hey Henry, this is Ricky. Remember me? Hey man, I got a problem. I was with some guys and they got high and started acting crazy so I got out of the car. I wouldn't bother you but I'm way out here in Three Points."

Carmen was yielding. Henry's hands were roaming freely over her body and she sagged lower on the couch. But the voice on the answering machine continued. "I got nobody else I can call, Dude, or I wouldn't bug you." A long pause followed, then, "Guess you're not there. Well man... um, sorry to bother you."

Henry let go of Carmen and picked up the phone. "Ricky?"

Ricky sounded small and weak. "Oh man, am I glad to hear your voice. I'm—"

"I heard the first part. Listen, Rick, call a cab and have them take you to my office. Johnson's on duty at the security gate. I'll call him and have him pay the driver."

"I already tried to get a cab. They said they won't send one out here."

Henry wasn't surprised. Three Points was a crossroads in the middle of desert scrub, almost forty miles from Tucson.

"I tried everything," Ricky said. "I wouldn't call you if I had any other way. But listen, I'll let you go. I gotta start walking."

"Wait a second." Henry cupped one hand over the phone and looked at Carmen. "How'd you like to take a little drive to a great place called Three Points?"

She had repositioned her dress and was staring at her champagne glass. "I've been to Three Points. That's where I grew up. Listen, Henry, I'm leaving on a plane at noon tomorrow so—"

"We'll be back in two hours."

"No... no thanks." Carmen held his gaze. Her lips parted as she slid her hand up his thigh.

Henry's body thrummed under the warmth of her touch, and at that moment he wanted her more than he'd ever wanted anything, but he stopped her hand and raised the phone to his ear. He started to speak, but his throat went dry. He tried to swallow, then licked his lips. Through his nearly closed throat, he said, "Rick, stay put. I'll be there."

While he got directions, he refilled Carmen's glass. He told Ricky he'd leave soon and set down the phone. Carmen moved to get up, but Henry put his hand on her shoulder.

"I have to use the bathroom," she said, brushing his hand away. "Can you wait till I'm finished peeing before you leave? Or are you in that big a hurry to get to Three Points?"

Henry moved to kiss her but she turned her head. He said, "Carmen, I can't just leave him stuck out there in the desert."

"Forget it, Henry."

When Henry stood up, his body ached and his knees wobbled. He pulled his car keys from his pants pocket. "Please lock the door when you leave."

Two hours later, he dropped Ricky off. On the way home, he passed a liquor store and thought he'd get a bottle of his favorite Scotch, but he knew he'd probably sit and mope about Carmen and drink half the bottle, so he kept driving

When he steered up the driveway to his house, he had the faint hope he'd see Carmen's car, but then he remembered she'd shipped it to Portland and had taken a cab to his place. He walked up the winding steps to his door, then stopped to look down on the grid of city lights.

He'd wondered, during the drive back, why he didn't feel the least bit noble about what he'd done. At first, he'd told himself it was because he knew that if he'd been a younger man, hormones pumping full-bore, Ricky would be walking home from Three Points. But as the truth came to him his face drooped and his shoulders sagged.

Henry cared deeply for Carmen, more than he'd cared for any woman he'd met in years, but the gulf in their ages was too wide. If he'd slept with her, her departure would have been even more wrenching. Ricky's call had given him a way out, and like any intelligent coward, he'd jumped at the chance to lessen his pain. He stood on the porch for a few minutes to fully absorb that unpleasant bit of self-information, and as he slid his key into the front door lock, he wondered whether the day would ever come when he'd stop learning things about himself that he really didn't want to know.

When he passed into the entryway, a sudden memory brought him the name of Carmen's perfume. To his empty living room, he whispered, "Shalimar... that's the name of that stuff," but he closed his mind in time to avoid the memory of the woman in his past who'd worn it. He tossed his keys on the coffee table, and as he crossed the room, something caught his attention. Carmen's satin dress was draped over the arm of a red leather chair. Her black high heels lay on the floor. A faint clicking sound, from the lid of that old Zippo, was echoing from down the hall.

He walked slowly down the hallway to his bedroom. It was lit by the glow of a candle, and Carmen lay in his bed. She was propped up on pillows, the sheet to her waist, her long, wavy hair covering her shoulders and breasts. In her left hand she held Ricky's lighter, and in her right, a champagne glass with an inch of wine remaining. She raised it to him, offering him the final sip. When Henry took the glass, she pulled her hair back and swept the sheet aside, displaying her lithe and sinuous body. Then she looked up at him and said, "Don't look so surprised. Did you really think I'd walk out on the noblest man I've ever met?"

Henry couldn't tell whether Carmen was sincere about his being noble or whether she just needed a ride to the airport the next day, but he decided that under the circumstances, it didn't really matter.

⊷⊶ ⊷⊶ ⊷⊶ ⊷⊶ ⊷⊶

PENURY

Mike King stood 5'4" and weighed about 140 lbs. He was meaner than a cornered snake and he loved to fight, and if he hadn't been that way, I wouldn't be alive to tell this story.

I never knew why the Garvey brothers would even bother with a kid like me. I still think they got me mixed up with somebody else. I'd been walking down Jefferson Street minding my own business when somebody said, "There he is!" and they grabbed me. A few minutes later, they had me at the end of a dead-end alley. I was on my knees, my chin resting on my chest, and through what was suddenly my one good eye, I watched my blood spill from my face onto the greasy bricks beneath my knees.

The Garveys were hoodlums. Steve had a long arrest record, and Dave was out on parole. The youngest one, Box, was quiet and dumb and did whatever his brothers told him. It was Steve who was standing over me. He had a knife in his right hand. He jerked my head back. My vision was blurred, but I remember seeing him move forward with that knife. I was fourteen at the time, and at that age, death is something that happened to old people. But now it was no longer an abstraction, and I went cold with fear. I'd never see my mom again or taste another Hershey bar. Just as Steve pressed the knife to my throat, a sound came from the end of the alley.

It was just a shout from out by the street, but Steve pulled the knife away and turned to look. My head dropped and I almost toppled over, but I still remember hearing the click of hard leather heels on those alley bricks. I turned to look but my focus was bad. A shape was coming toward us, and all the Garveys had turned to face it.

The shape didn't say anything, but went straight at Steve. Steve swung the knife wildly, putting himself off balance, and caught a vicious kick to the ribs. He staggered forward and went down, but before he could get up the other guy pivoted like a field goal kicker and kicked Steve in the gut. That was it for Steve. He heaved forward and curled up, moaning. Then he got one more kick to the side of the head and he stopped moaning.

The guy who'd kicked him turned toward me and I recognized him. It was Mike King. He shouldn't have diverted his attention to me.

Dave Garvey had been too shocked to react at first, but he had a steel pipe and he hit King hard on the left shoulder.

King staggered, but he spun around and caught Dave with a kick to the kneecap. Dave stumbled, then regained his balance. He came at King again with the pipe, but King, being so much shorter, dodged to one side, swung his right leg up, and caught Dave deep in the crotch.

Dave's eyes got big and he wobbled, dropping the pipe. It clanged as it struck the bricks and started to roll away.

King picked it up, hefted it like a baseball bat, and was ready to swing at Dave's head when he heard footsteps clicking up the alley. It was Box, running away. King glanced at Dave, who was on one knee spilling his guts. He dropped the pipe and took off after Box.

Halfway up the alley he caught him. Like I said, I was having a hard time seeing, but it looked like King jumped on Box's back. Box fell on his face and let out a grunt. King straddled Box like he was a horse and pinned his right arm behind his back. Then he lifted the elbow, leaned back, and with all his weight shoved the elbow forward. It made a funny sound, like somebody snapping a pencil underwater. Box let out a squeal.

King got to his feet. He rubbed his left shoulder and tried to raise his arm but couldn't. He drew back his foot, ready to kick Box in the head. Then he looked back at me.

I was trying to get to my feet. My nose was smashed, my lips were split, one of my eyes was swollen shut, and my front teeth were loose. The blood was clogging me up, and I couldn't seem to get any air. I tipped my head back and looked up at a dirty white sign that read *Deliveries*, its hand-painted letters written in dripping black paint. I tried to focus on it, wanting to get my right eye to work.

A hand closed on my arm. "Can you walk?" King said.

I opened my mouth, but nothing came out. Keeping his grip on my arm, he helped me out of the alley. We walked past Box, who was bawling and trying to roll over. King chugged up a wad of phlegm from his throat and spat. The pearly-green glob landed on Box' pockmarked cheek, but I don't think he noticed.

At the street, King looked closely at me. He asked whether I lived nearby and I said yes. He said he'd help me home, but I was getting a bit steadier on my feet, so I told him I'd be okay. I was just about to tell him thanks when we heard the low rumble of exhaust pipes and a green '56 Chevy pulled over.

King glanced at it, then asked me if I wanted a ride, but I said I could make it home okay. He stood there, shorter and skinnier than me, with his crew-cut blond hair and bony cheeks, looking up at me with his cold grey eyes. He had a bent nose and a purple scar over his right eye, and his skin was flushed from the heat of the fight, but his breathing was easy.

I wanted to kneel at his feet, but he jumped into the green Chevy and was gone before I could get any words out. I watched the Chevy drive off, and I still remember the rap of its exhaust echoing down the cold, empty street.

My mom almost fainted when I got home, and it was three weeks before I went back to school. I went to Central Catholic, the same school King went to. I saw him in the hallway several times and wanted to go up to him and thank him for what he'd done, but I was a freshman and King was a senior, and freshmen didn't just walk up to seniors and start a conversation. That was considered a gesture of disrespect.

The rest of the spring semester, I tried to find a way to talk to him, but when we passed in the hallway he didn't even acknowledge me. Whenever I saw him, I had a feeling of reverence I never got from any of the religion they taught me.

All of this happened a long time ago, though I'm reminded of it daily when I look in the mirror and see the crooked nose that's part of the landscape of my face. But the whole ugly story came fresh to my mind just recently, when I went back home for Thanksgiving.

There's a bar, the Ace of Clubs, just a block away from where the Garveys jumped me. I hadn't been there in twenty years, but I passed it on my way from the airport and decided to stop in. The place hadn't changed. It was smoky and dingy, and the toilet still threatened to overflow when you flushed. Even the crowd was the same, just older and sadder.

I had said my hellos to everybody at the bar and was on my third beer when somebody down the bar mentioned Box Garvey. I knew that Dave and Steve were both dead, but I'd never heard what happened to Box. The place was noisy, so all I heard was something about Box being "sent up for good this time."

I took another drink from my beer and looked across at the mirror behind the bar. I felt a twinge in my nose, then brushed my tongue over my front teeth, and the whole scene came back to me, played in fast forward. I saw Mike King in my mind as clearly as the day it had happened, that hard face of his washed by the blue glare of the streetlight. I glanced at the guy sitting next to me at the bar. It was Phil Commons, who was a couple years older than me and a graduate of Central Catholic. "Hey Phil, you remember Mike King?"

"Hell yeah, I remember him. Greatest wrestler Central ever had. City and State Champ four years in a row. Won twenty straight matches without a point being scored on him. He was undefeated, except for one match. And he got screwed on that one."

I couldn't imagine that. "Who beat him?"

"He didn't get beat. He had to forfeit. I remember. I was there."

My beer was warm, but my throat was dry and the smoke was getting to me, so I drained it. Then I set the damp bottle down. "What happened?"

"Well, King took off his warm-up jacket and walked out on the mat. His left shoulder was black all over, and it was swollen real big. The referee said something and King tried to raise his arm, but he could hardly lift it. Coach Purvis came out on the mat and the ref said something to him. Purvis looked at King's shoulder and pointed to the showers, but King just stood there. His face got beet-red. He followed Purvis off the mat, saying something nobody could hear. When they got to the bench Purvis spun around and pointed to the lockers. I remember how quiet the gym was. The ref raised the arm of the guy King was supposed to wrestle, but nobody cheered. It was ugly."

Another beer appeared in front of me, but I didn't want it. The taste in my mouth was so sour no beer could wash it away. Mike King had only one blemish on his wrestling record, and he had gotten it because he was hurt while saving me from the Garvey brothers. But he'd never said a word about it to me, and for reasons I can't fathom, I hadn't heard about it at the time. Maybe because I was out of school for awhile, or maybe because I was too absorbed in my own drama. A drop of sweat slid down the side of the beer bottle. I wanted water, and lots of it, but then I wanted something a lot more than water. "Whatever happened to King?"

Phil stuck a pretzel in his mouth and chewed. "He got a wrestling scholarship to Purdue. He was so smart he could'a got one on his grades, but he joined the Army instead. Went straight to Vietnam and did two tours. When he got out, he married Peggy Hennessey. She was about your age, I think." He was right about that. Peggy had graduated the same year I did. She was drop-dead lovely and her daddy was loaded. "Anyway, she and Mike moved to Zionsville and started a horse farm."

I was peeling the soggy label off the beer bottle with my thumbnail, trying to remember how to get to Zionsville. "I'd like to look him up. Is Zionsville straight up Michigan Road?"

Phil took a sip from a shot glass and followed it with a drink of beer. He looked across the bar at my reflection. We watched each other's image in the nicotine-coated glass as I waited. After a long moment Phil said, "He ain't in Zionsville, but I know where you can find him. He's in Holy Cross Cemetery. He died of cancer about a year ago. The Viet Cong couldn't kill him, but Agent Orange did."

I kept staring at my reflection across the bar. The cigarette smoke hung in flat clouds and stung my eyes and blurred my vision, but I could still see Mike King standing in front of me at the end of that alley, looking up with that squint-eyed stare, his left shoulder a little lower than his right.

I tried to pay for my rounds of beer, but the bartender said they'd been paid for. I said thanks to the room in general as I left, hoping the buyer heard me. I stepped out the door and down the crumbling concrete steps, and the shock of the frozen November air slapped me awake. I looked down the street at that mean old alley. All the dark, sooty buildings were just as they had been so many years ago, frozen in time like the inside of the Ace of Clubs Bar. The cold was seeping through my thin jacket, so I hurried to my rental car and drove through the dark, silent streets, out to far the eastern suburbs where my sister lived.

The next day was overcast and windy. I bought flowers at a grocery store and drove through Holy Cross Cemetery, following the little map they'd given me at the sales office. I found the spot where they said to park, and when I got out, I remembered why I'd moved to a warmer climate. The wind scoured my face, and it had started to snow. I knew the bad weather was just beginning, and long gloomy months loomed ahead.

The gravestone was hard to find because it was a flat bronze plate. In raised letters it read,

Lt. Michael T. King
U. S. Army
Nov 27, 1948 – Dec 12, 2009

I thought it was a meager monument for a man of his moral stature, and it took me a moment to realize that the date of that very day was November 27.

A sickly gray feeling crept into me, a memory of long-forgotten shame. I knew I was a hopeless debtor, with an account I could never repay. I'd come into the world in a state of arrears, and all I'd done was accumulate debt. As I stood over Mike King's grave, watching the snow blow across the frostbitten grass, I knew exactly where I'd be on this date every year until it was my turn to die.

I stuffed the flowers into the thin metal vase beside the grave. The bright red petals quivered in the wind, and I knew they'd be frozen soon. But there would be flowers on this grave every November 27th from that day on, and though it was a pathetic gesture that Mike King himself would've laughed at, it was all I could do.

As I walked back to my car, I made a list in my mind. I had people to see and thanks to give, and I knew I'd better get my flight moved back a few days. There was a lot that needed to be said, and I was going to say it while there was still time.

THE PERFECT COLOR

Elaine Benning never left a drawer hanging open. Never.

When she came home one afternoon and saw the vanity drawer half-open in her downstairs bathroom, she knew someone had been in her house.

Or was still there.

She stifled her panic and listened. The only sound was the grandfather clock ticking in the hallway. The steady rhythm seemed uncommonly loud in the stillness.

She thought to call the police, but what if the intruder heard her call? Her purse was hanging on her arm, and she felt the weight of the heavy revolver she'd carried since her husband had died. She pulled out the shiny gun and eased the hammer back, then tiptoed through the house, holding the gun in front of her, checking closets and bathrooms.

Nobody there. She considered running out the door, but cold anger overcame her. *This is my house, by God!* She started up the stairway, timing her steps to match alternating ticks of the old clock.

Her bedroom was first on the left. She eased through the doorway and scanned the room. Something seemed odd about her dressing table. Then she noticed the closet doors. They were bifold doors and they often jammed, so she never closed them, but they were closed now. She knelt beside her bed, leaned forward, and aimed the revolver at the doors. "I know you're in there. I've got a gun. Open the doors slowly and come out or I'll start shooting."

Nothing happened. She started to think she was crazy. *Could I have closed the doors myself? No way. There has to be someone in there. Should I just start shooting? What if it's some kid? What if it's a drug-crazed psychopath?*

She waited a few more seconds and raised the gun. "Come out now, or I'll shoot."

"Okay," a man said, his voice muffled by the doors. "I'll come out. Don't shoot." The doors creaked open and a man stepped out. He was medium height, slender, and dressed in black.

Elaine held the gun steady, despite her heaving chest. *What do I do now?* she thought. She looked closely at his face. *Why does he seem so familiar?* Struggling to sound calm, she said, "What do you want?"

The man pointed to a plastic bag on the floor. "Those things."

"What's in there?"

"Your makeup... and some underwear."

She looked again at her dresser top. It had been swept clean of her makeup items, but her gold Rolex was still there. It was a treasured memento, but she never wore it. "Why didn't you take the watch?"

"I already have a lady's watch."

She studied his face. She knew him; she was sure of it. "Why do you want to steal makeup and underwear?"

He lowered his eyes. "I wanted to… use it. I'm too embarrassed to buy it myself."

Elaine didn't know whether to sneer or laugh. "So you want to dress up like a lady and put on makeup, is that it?"

He nodded. "I've always been able to fight the urge, but my wife is divorcing me. My life's falling apart. I don't have the strength to fight it anymore."

"Why'd you break in here? I mean why'd you pick my house?"

"I know you're in real estate. You're gone a lot." He shrugged. "I thought it was the best choice."

Now she remembered who he was. His name was Richard, and he was a member of her country club. "Well, you picked the wrong house. You scared the living hell out of me and you're gonna pay for it."

"You can call the police if you want. I won't run away. Or you could do the merciful thing: you could shoot me."

She kept the gun pointed at his chest. From this range, she couldn't miss. Her finger twitched on the trigger. She was trying desperately to hate the man. "All right, you want the merciful thing, you'll get it." She raised the gun and pointed it at his head. "Sit down in that chair."

He lowered his hands and sat down in front of her dresser. He faced the mirror and closed his eyes.

Elaine moved up beside him. She leaned near him, and he cringed. With her left hand, she opened a dresser drawer and pulled out a large burgundy-colored case. She set the case on the dressing table and laid it open. She tossed the gun on the bed, and from a row of a dozen lipsticks, she extracted one and opened it. She said, "Open your eyes." She looked closely at his blue eyes and tanned skin and held the lipstick near his face. "This one's called Morning Magenta. For you, my dear, it's the perfect color."

She went to work on his face. She cleansed, rubbed, smoothed, dabbed and patted. She penciled his eyebrows and lined his eyelids, then brushed his eyelashes until they were long and dark. "And now," she said, "the lips." When she leaned closer to apply the lipstick, she saw a tear welling in the corner of his eye. She put her hand to his chin. "No tears allowed, Dear. They'll smear your mascara."

When she finished with his lips, she stood back to look at him. "Now, for the final touch." She went into the closet and returned with a wig, a long, lustrous crown of wavy black hair. She laid it gently on his head and smoothed it. She adjusted the long strands to fall over his shoulders. "My deceased husband bought this for me. Isn't it beautiful? There are five others, all different shades." She stood away from the mirror. Richard was alone in it.

He looked at himself for a few seconds, then raised his hand to caress and fluff the dark hair. He turned his head from side to side, then looked up at Elaine and smiled. "What do you think of me as a woman?"

"You look lovely." She stood behind him again, her hands resting on his shoulders, looking at their reflection. Her fair skin and blonde hair contrasted with his dark features, but their eyes were the same shade of blue.

"I know your name is Richard, but I'd feel odd calling you that while you're in makeup. If you were a woman, what name would you choose?"

He studied his reflection in the mirror. "I've always liked Vanessa."

Elaine leaned forward and pressed her cheek to his. "Hello Vanessa."

"Hello Elaine."

They moved to sit near the fireplace in the sitting area of the bedroom. Elaine did most of the talking, telling her new friend about the struggles of being a woman on her own, of the good living she was making, and of the boorish men she encountered. Richard laughed, a girlish laugh, like a younger sister listening to prom tales. Elaine cancelled her afternoon appointments, and they talked until dark. They made a date to meet again two days later.

Their visits grew regular and frequent. Elaine found herself looking forward to them. She entered their meetings as *Vanessa* in her schedule book, and never allowed business to conflict with their time together. During one of their morning sessions, they were sitting at the kitchen table, both in their bathrobes.

"Vanessa, you never talk about your divorce. Is it too painful to talk about?"

Richard sipped his coffee and set his cup down. "Doris is handling the whole thing. I'll just be signing papers. What bothers me most is the pain it's causing our daughter, Maria. She just turned 13, and she's falling apart over this. We've always been close, and she hates the prospect of living with Doris.

"As for myself, I don't really know what I feel. Since I work for my father-in-law, I'll surely lose my job. And I still love Doris... at least I think I do. I just don't know." He raised his hand to wipe away a tear. "Elaine, I know I'm a mess, but having you for a friend is a huge relief. You know my ugly secret and you don't despise me."

Elaine laid her hand on his. "Why is it ugly? What's the harm? Are we hurting anyone?"

"Maybe ugly isn't the right word, but I'm still a man at heart, and I wonder what kind of man would do what I've been doing with you."

She pressed her other hand on his. They seldom touched, their only contact being in the makeup process, but she couldn't deny herself this gesture. "We're friends, Vanessa. If this makes us happy, what else matters?"

He pushed his cup aside, and with his fingers he traced the veins on the back of her warm hand. "You're right. What else matters?"

Elaine went away for a week on business, and she missed Richard deeply. Or was it Vanessa she missed? When they met again they embraced for the first time. It was a long embrace, and it startled her. If Richard hadn't edged away first, she wondered what she would have done.

She'd bought him a new robe, and after she applied his makeup, she coiffed him in a brunette wig, and he went to sit by the fire. Elaine slipped into a revealing nightgown. When she looked in the mirror, she felt embarrassed for Richard to see her flat chest and bony figure—though she was almost 40, she still looked like a boy with breasts—but when she sat next to Vanessa, the feeling disappeared. She leaned close to pour some wine, and their knees touched. A rush of blood flushed the skin of her neck. She knew that if her friend didn't make the first move, she would. They clinked glasses, and when their eyes met, she braced herself for a kiss.

But Richard had something on his mind. "I saw Doris last week," he said. "She had some surprising things to say. She... she wants to get back together."

Elaine almost spilled her wine. "After all the things she's said to you? After everything she's done? How can she even think you'd want to be with her?"

"I'm as surprised as you are."

"What changed her mind?"

"I'll tell you what she said, but I've got no explanation for it. She said I've changed. She said that in the last few weeks she's looked forward to our meetings at the attorneys. She says I look different. If she saw what I look like now, my God...."

They laughed.

"I think she's full of shit," he said. "If anyone's changed it's her, but I can't explain that either. I do know she's no longer a force in my life. I'm not exactly sure what that means, and I don't care."

Elaine sipped her wine. She wished they had kissed before he'd had a chance to talk. Finally she said, "How do you think she'd react if she knew of our meetings? Do you think she might know? Maybe she's jealous."

"I don't think she knows, and I don't care if she finds out."

Elaine smiled, but her friend didn't notice. He was looking out the window, his mind far away.

At their next meeting, Elaine showed Richard a new gown she had bought him. It was silky, low-cut, and very sheer. He held it in front of him as he looked at himself in the mirror. "It's beautiful, Elaine." He lowered his arms slowly, tucked the gown back in its box, and put the lid on it.

Something cold stung Elaine's heart. "Don't you like it?"

"It's perfect... but something's changed."

"You're going back to her."

"I am, but on my terms. We were together last night. I have to tell you about it." He sat down on the bed, reached for her hand, and pulled her down beside him. "Doris has never been a passionate woman, but it seems there's something about me now that gets her all fired up. I leaned closer to kiss her goodbye last night and she almost collapsed in my arms. We went upstairs. For four hours I treated her like a cheap whore, and she just begged for more."

"You think she's serious?"

"She cancelled our final meeting with the attorneys. She says it's my call now. She bought a huge new bed, and we've had separate bedrooms for two years." He laid his hand on the gift box. "I... I can't go on with this."

"Are you going to let guilt get in the way again?"

"It's not guilt," he said, his eyes scanning the sparkling bottles on her dressing table. "I just don't need it anymore. I always believed if I went through with my fantasy, I'd just die of shame… but I didn't die. That's the only explanation I can think of."

Elaine put her hand to her mouth and turned her head. He touched her shoulder, but she pulled away from him.

"Elaine, I owe you so much. It makes me sick to hurt you. You've done more for me than anyone in my life. You gave me *back* my life, in a way. Elaine, I'm so sorry."

She wiped her eyes. "I think I understand, Vaness—I mean… Richard." She took a handkerchief from her pocket and dabbed the melting mascara from her cheeks.

Richard put his hand on her knee. "I'll always be here for you, just like you were for me, and if there's anything I can ever do for you, just ask."

"Oh stop that." She brushed his hand away and scooted sideways on the bed. "I did this for my own reasons. You were… well, I mean… I never had a sister." She got up first, and he followed her downstairs. At the front doorway, they embraced, neither of them caring whether they were seen from the street.

"I wish you luck, Richard."

"Thanks. And remember, if there's anything I can do for you, don't hesitate to ask." He turned to leave.

She grabbed the sleeve of his jacket. "Wait. Come to think of it, there might be something you could do." She glanced sideways and spoke in a whisper. "There's a big tennis tournament coming to the club next month, isn't there?"

"Yes. All the big names'll be there."

"Aren't you the Tournament Chairman?"

He smiled and nodded. "Yes, unfortunately. I'm responsible for everything from the condition of the courts to the color of the attendants' uniforms. You don't have to worry about tickets. I'll get you courtside seats if you want."

"No, I don't want tickets. I—" She couldn't seem to get the words out.

"Fess up, girl. What's on your mind?"

"Well, ever since I was a teenager, I've had this weird fantasy. I've wanted to sneak into a men's locker room... you know, when they're all getting showers? I have a friend who's a makeup artist, and if I get my hair cut really short and get the right kind of glasses, do you think—"

Richard held up his hand. "Say no more. Remember I said I had to pick the color of the attendants' uniforms?"

Elaine nodded.

He kissed her tenderly on the corner of her mouth. "There's one shade, I think it's called Sunset Blue. For you, my dear, it's the perfect color."

Six Men

Ray knew he was driving too fast. The rear wheels of his truck slid sideways in the turn, skidding over the greasy mud and loose gravel. Twice he'd almost lost control, but a monsoon storm was building behind him and it was moving faster than he was, so he kept on at the same speed. If the storm caught him and the washes flooded any worse, they'd be stuck.

He glanced at Phil. The veins in Phil's neck were throbbing and his sun-dried face had a sour look. Ray said, "If we don't get to the highway before this storm hits, we'll be stuck out here. You wanna spend the night in the desert?"

"No, but I want to get back to Tucson alive. Next time we come down here to check a job, I'm bringing whiskey and a tent."

Ray checked his side mirror. The shroud of black clouds was closing in, about to overtake him. He knew this road by heart. The next turn was a wide one, so he held his speed. Halfway around it, the rear wheels kicked away to his right and he barely missed slamming into a boulder. He regained control and gassed down hard, but when he rounded the bend there was something in the middle of the road.

At first it was a jumble of shapes, hard to make out in the half-dark, but as he slammed on the brakes and skidded, he saw it was a group of men. They were startled by the sudden appearance of the truck and jumped to the side of the road. Ray slid to a stop near the group, then slowly eased forward.

There were six of them, dressed in jeans and plaid shirts, the tallest wearing a denim jacket. They were wearing ball caps and carrying small backpacks, but this wasn't a group of hikers.

"Illegals," Phil said.

Ray stopped the truck and rolled down his window. The man in the denim jacket stepped forward and took off his cap, uncovering shiny, jet-black hair. His dark, leathery face made his white teeth look fluorescent, and he squinted his pale blue eyes against the wind. He flipped a small salute and smiled.

Ray kept the truck running and in gear. "*Que pasa, hombre?*"

The man dropped his hand to his side and put it in his pocket. "*Nada, señor,*" he said. He was trying to look calm, but Ray could tell the guy was nervous. In his other hand, the man held a plastic water bottle. It was half-full with a cloudy brown liquid. *Creek water*, Ray thought. He motioned toward the rear of the truck. "Agua?"

The tall man didn't move, but one of the younger guys stepped to the back of the truck, to the orange cooler strapped behind the bed. He bent and let the water drain onto his face. After he took a few gulps, one of the others said something and nudged him aside. Ray heard angry words as he watched this in his mirror. The man in the denim jacket went to the back of the truck and spoke quietly. The men formed a line behind the water jug, dumped the creek water from their plastic bottles and refilled them from the cooler. The tall one was the last to drink.

The wind picked up. The air was rich with the smell of rain, and a heavy roll of thunder rumbled in from the south. Vertical lightning split the grey sky, followed by a shattering boom.

"Let's go," Phil said.

Ray flipped on the headlights. "Hold on. I'll be right back."

He got out and stood beside the truck. The tall man came forward and said, in clear English, "Señor, is this the road to Phoenix?"

Ray stifled a laugh. "No, man, you got to get to the highway, then go north."

"How much more miles?"

"About two hundred and fifty."

The man moved back a step. He turned his head, then looked at the ground, trying to hide his disbelief.

Ray said, "Where you guys from?"

The man didn't answer right away, then he looked directly at Ray and said, "Guadalajara."

Another white bolt flashed in the southern sky. Ray needed to get moving, but he hesitated. "You guys want a ride to the highway?"

"How much money?"

Ray pointed to the back of the truck. "No money. Get in."

The tall man spoke to the others. They jumped up into the truck bed and snuggled among the tools and lumber. When they were settled, as Ray reached to shift gears, Phil grabbed his arm. "What the hell you doing, man? The ranchers around here call the Border Patrol when they see illegals. They could be on their way right now. We get caught with these guys we're screwed."

Ray looked in the mirror. The six men were hunched together behind the cab. The rain started, the fat drops exploding on the windshield. "Relax. We'll drop them off near the highway at that old cow shed. They can stay there till the Border Patrol finds them."

"But if the Border Patrol catches us hauling these guys, they'll let them go and put us in jail. That don't sound to me like a risk worth taking."

Ray hunched forward, staring into the windshield. The rain was slamming against the glass, and even with the wipers flapping at full speed, it was like driving underwater.

"I'm telling you Ray, this is a mistake. Last week a guy in Sierra Vista got two years in prison for helping illegals."

Ray slowed the truck and looked over at Phil. "We couldn't run this roofing business without illegals, and you know it. You want to get up there on those roofs and mop that hot tar?"

"But our guys got good papers. These guys are fresh from the border."

Ray glared at Phil. "You say one more fucking word, it'll be you that walks, not them."

The truck wallowed across two more flooded washes, and a half-hour later they were nearing the Sonoita highway. Ray pulled up by a leaning cow-shed under a clump of mesquite trees. He set the emergency brake and got out. He pointed to the shed and spoke to the man in the denim jacket. The rain fell slow and steady, dripping from the brims of their hats.

"You can wait there till the rain stops. Be careful. La Migre comes by here all the time."

The man squinted, looking at the shed. He looked back at Ray. "Thank you for your kindness. If we walk north, we will someday get to Phoenix?"

"Better stay off the highway. The border patrol—" Ray stopped talking. He knew the best thing for these guys was to get picked up by the Border Patrol. Wandering around in this storm they could get struck by lightning. "Gotta go," he said. "Good luck."

The other man mumbled something, but a clap of thunder drowned his words. Ray got in the truck and pulled away.

Phil let out a long sigh. He pushed back the cap that covered his stringy blond hair and wiped sweat from his face.

Ray looked at him. "Feel better?"

Phil nodded. "The Border Patrol will pick 'em up soon, and that'll be that. Back to old Mexico, where they belong."

Ray didn't comment. He'd had this discussion with Phil and a hundred other people far too many times. As far as they were concerned, the little brown people should stay where they belonged. But it was the little brown people who did the dirty work that Chicanos were too proud and gringos were too lazy to do, and they lived in constant fear of arrest and deportation. That didn't seem to matter to anyone. It pissed Ray off every time he talked about it, so he kept quiet. Besides, he'd never convinced anybody.

But he'd kept his eye on his mirror as he pulled away slowly, watching the six men. They hadn't gone to the shed. They remained clustered in the middle of the road; then one of them pointed toward the highway and Ray lost sight of them in the rain and the darkness.

As they approached the stop sign near the highway, a pale green Border Patrol van came from the north.

"Here they come, just like I told you," said Phil. "I bet they're looking for our passengers."

The van had its wig-wag lights on, and the driver blinked his high-beams as he approached, but he didn't slow down. He sped straight past them down the highway.

"Looks like they've got other fish to fry," Ray said. He kept his foot on the brake and his eyes on the rearview mirror. He knew what he was about to see. Over the rise of a small hill, he saw the six men walking toward him. They were bunched together, almost hidden in the mist. He turned to look at Phil.

"Have we got that big green tarp with us, the one we picked up at Miller's Surplus"?

Phil looked back and saw the six men. "You're out of your mind, man."

Ray checked his watch, then shifted into Reverse and gave Phil a hard stare. "These guys come all the way up here from Guadalajara. Their Coyote dumped them in the middle of nowhere. They got no food, almost no money, and they've been drinking muddy water. They know its 250 miles to Phoenix, but they're still walking, even in this godawful storm."

"That ain't our problem."

"I'm making it my problem. They came all this way to get to Phoenix, and by God they're gonna get there." When he got to the men, he pulled to the side of the road. The taller man walked toward the truck.

Ray got out. "You guys want a ride to Phoenix?"

"*Sí*... I mean yes. You know we have no much money for the gas."

"I don't want any money. But you'll have to ride for a while under a tarp. We get to Tucson, I can get another vehicle and drive you up to Phoenix."

One of the other men, an old man, came to their side. He asked what was going on. The tall man told him of Ray's offer. The old man looked at Ray and smiled. He was thin and pale. His breathing was labored, and his vein-streaked hand shook as he tipped his hat.

It took five minutes to get them situated under the stiff green canvas. Ray laid some shovels and a few shingles over them and pulled away, waiting for Phil to say something.

Phil remained quiet. The rain pounding the windshield was the only sound other than the hissing of the tires.

"We'll be back in Tucson by 5 o'clock," Ray said. "Want me to drop you at the office, or you want to take a little ride up to Phoenix with me?"

"How you gonna get them to Phoenix? All the trucks are on other jobs. You gonna haul them up there wrapped in canvas?"

Ray had to think for a minute. "I'll take the Suburban. Mona should be home by now."

Phil chuckled. "She'll love that. Six wet, dirty Mexicans riding on her leather seats."

An hour later they pulled up at the office of Pueblo Roofing. Ray parked beside a metal shed and killed the engine.

"Start at the usual time tomorrow?" Phil asked. Ray nodded.

"If you're in jail, want me to look after things?"

Ray nodded again, then stepped out of the truck. The six men had jumped down.

Five of them were wringing out their wet shirts, but the old man was alone, his arms wrapped around him. They all waved at Phil as he drove away in his red pickup, but Phil didn't notice.

The cool air startled Ray as he stepped into his office. He checked the phone messages, scribbled a note for his secretary, and called Mona, his wife. She didn't answer, so he left a voicemail saying he'd be home soon.

As he was locking the office door, he heard footsteps behind him. It was the tall man in the denim jacket.

"My name is Diego," he said, extending his hand. "Where are we?"

Ray shook the man's hand. It was hard, dry and calloused. "I'm Ray Gooding. This is my office. You still want to go to Phoenix?"

Diego nodded.

"Here's the plan. We'll go to my house and pick up another vehicle. It takes a couple hours to get to Phoenix, depending on traffic. Do you have any connections up there, anybody to contact?"

Diego went back to the others and spoke to the old man, who reached into his jacket for something and handed it to Diego. Diego patted the old man on the shoulder and returned to Ray, handing him a tattered envelope. "Can you take us to this place?"

It was a letter addressed to Manuel Santa Cruz, Guadalajara, Mexico, but the return address was in Rancho Vista Estates in Phoenix. Ray knew where it was. Despite the fancy name, it was a sprawling trailer park on the south side of town.

"Okay, that's where we'll go. Tell the hombres to get in."

Twenty minutes later Ray steered into his driveway. His wife's white Suburban wasn't there, so he was surprised to see her standing at the wide picture window of the living room. He shut off the engine and told the men to wait in the garage.

He was greeted at the kitchen door by his two young daughters. They both had new toys to show him. When Mona walked in, he smelled the perfume of her body and almost forgot he was in a hurry. She kissed him on the cheek and took his hand.

He was about to return the kiss but stopped short. "Where's the Suburban?"

"At the dealer. It's the brakes again. They said it'd be ready by five tomorrow. Were you thinking of taking your wife and daughters out to dinner? We could all squeeze into the front of the truck."

"Sorry, Babe. I gotta run up to Phoenix."

His daughters, blonds like their mother, tugged at his jeans, trying to get his attention. A long rumble of thunder came from the south.

"Who're those guys in the garage?" Mona asked, ignoring the ringing phone.

"Just some guys."

"If they're new employees, I hope they've got documentation."

"Don't worry."

He pulled away and went to the bedroom. He put on dry jeans and a white T shirt, took a wad of money from a jar he kept under the bed and went back to the kitchen.

Mona was standing in the same spot, arms folded across her pale blue sundress, looking through the door at the six Mexicans. "Ray, what's going on?"

He sat down to lace his boots. He finished tying one and looked up, straight into Mona's steel-grey eyes. "They're illegals. I'm giving them a ride to Phoenix."

Thunder rolled again. The storm Ray had fled was moving into town. Mona flipped a light switch but she didn't say anything. Ray was glad. He didn't have any good answers.

He finished tying his boots and went to the refrigerator. He took out a loaf of bread, a jar of grape jelly, and a gallon of milk. He took some paper cups from the cabinet and a jar of peanut butter from the pantry. Mona watched, then handed him a knife from the drawer. When he grabbed it she held onto it. "What if you get caught?"

"You know me, Mona. I don't get caught."

"That's because you're always careful. This is stupid. You can't go riding around with... are you taking them in your truck? It's going to storm again."

Ray pulled the knife again and she let go of it. He moved to kiss her but she backed away.

"Don't do this, Ray. Please."

He set the food on the kitchen counter and put his hands on her shoulders. "I told these guys I'd take them to Phoenix, and that's what I'm gonna do. I'll be back here by eleven o'clock. Don't worry."

He let go of her and hurried into the garage. The six men were standing in a circle, two of them smoking. Ray offered them the food and motioned for Diego to step aside. He spoke quietly so the others couldn't hear. "My family car's in the shop. I don't have another vehicle to spare. If you want to go, you'll have to ride all the way to Phoenix under that tarp."

Diego pushed his hat back and smiled. "It is very good to have the tarp. It will be much better than to be in the rain."

"What about that old guy? He looks pretty shaky."

"You no worry of Manuel. We take care for him."

Twenty minutes later, the men were under the tarp and lying side by side, with two stretched sideways across the back of the truck bed. As Ray pulled out of the driveway, Mona was watching from the picture window. He waved to her, but she didn't wave back.

It took a half-hour to get to the freeway. Traffic was heavy and slow, and it was another half-hour before the lights of Tucson began to fade. Just as his speed hit 75, Ray saw a stream of taillights flash red. He had to hit his brakes hard, and the line of traffic slowed to a crawl. Ten minutes passed before he was close enough to see what had happened.

A rusted Ryder box van was capsized on the grass beside the road. Two state policemen were standing beside a man who was handcuffed to the bumper. Nearby, men sat clustered in groups of three or four. They were dark-skinned men, like those in the back of Ray's truck, and they were sitting with their heads bowed, arms folded around their knees. Three long shapes lay stretched on the grass, shrouded in white cloth.

Traffic had squeezed into one lane, creeping along so every driver could get a good look at the scene. A pair of Border Patrolmen were standing beside the road, watching each vehicle that passed. Ray felt his engine sputter. He shifted to neutral, pressed on the accelerator, and glanced at his fuel gauges. Both tanks read Empty.

He was ten feet from the accident when the line stopped. The two Border Patrolmen had stopped a vehicle and were looking it over. Ray looked at his load. One of the men had sat up and was looking around. Ray hammered on the glass and motioned for him to get down, but then the line moved ahead. As Ray edged forward, he looked straight into the face of one of the Border Patrol guys. He felt his neck stiffen and his mouth go dry. He eased on through and didn't look back. When his speed reached 70, he looked at himself in his rearview mirror.

A rush of adrenaline stung his heart, then came a sharp twist in his gut. He realized in an instant what he was really doing. He'd started this foolish escapade with the lame illusion that he was doing something noble, but it had nothing to do with helping six illegals get to Phoenix. He knew now it was just his own way of giving the finger to the heartless gray-suit mob, the ones who considered laws on paper and lines on maps to be the only true realities. To them, the people who had to struggle within those lines weren't real, they were just bothersome numbers. Ray hated the gray-suit bastards, but he knew he'd risked too much for a pathetic gesture of defiance. He looked again at his image in the mirror.

"You're a fool," he said. But he wasn't turning back, and he wasn't dumping the six Mexicans beside the road. Unless fate intervened, he was taking them to Phoenix, if it cost him all he had.

Sweat oozed between his fingers, and he squeezed the wheel so hard his knuckles ached. He stared into the rain-smeared windshield, looking for the exit sign for Toltec Plaza. The Border Patrol was thick as hell around Toltec, but he had to get fuel. He turned to check his cargo. They were covered. He drove slow to save fuel, waiting for the telltale stumble in the engine, but it didn't come and he eased off at the Toltec exit. There were two gas stations on the east side. The one on the right was less busy. He pulled up to the end pump and left the motor running.

Headlights flashed behind him. He checked his side mirror. Two white vans with green side-stripes pulled in at the opposite side of the pumps. The first one pulled even with Ray's truck and stopped. It was a Border Patrol van, with two patrolmen inside.

Ray couldn't turn to see whether his men were covered, so he lowered his mirror. Two faces were visible, and all the bodies were squirming. He rapped on the glass, but it was too late to say anything. He had to refuel and he had to look cool and natural doing it, so he got out of the truck.

The Border Patrol guys were filling their tanks. One of them was standing off from the rest, drinking from a Styrofoam cup. He was scanning the other vehicles in the plaza. He looked in Ray's direction.

Ray stood at the pump, sliding his credit card into the machine. The sign flashed *See Attendant*. He tried again with the same result. A voice from the loudspeaker said, "Sir, could you please come inside?"

Ray was searching for another card when he looked up and saw the Border patrolman walking toward him. The guy was tall and lean. His wide-brimmed hat was tipped forward, so Ray couldn't see his eyes. He walked to the front of Ray's truck, stopped, and put his hand on the hood.

"They have this problem all the time," he said. "They have to run the credit card manually, so you have to go inside."

Ray looked over at the Border Patrol guys. They were filling their tanks.

"We don't use cards; we got a special number we punch in."

"Can I borrow it?" Ray asked, straining to appear casual.

The Border Patrolman smiled, but Ray still couldn't see his eyes. Then the guy started to move forward.

Ray pulled the nozzle from the truck and returned it to the pump. "Looks crowded in the store. Guess I'll try somewhere else."

He squirmed into the truck, backed away, and steered out of the plaza. There was another gas station across the road, but it was jammed with vehicles waiting at every pump. The only choice was the truck plaza across the highway bridge. Ray pulled out and headed that way, but traffic on the freeway was slow, and there was a line of vehicles backed up, waiting to get on. Ray watched his mirror as the Border Patrol vehicles joined the line behind him

When traffic cleared he started across the bridge. He looked up and down the freeway.

Traffic was slow in both directions. As he crossed, one of the Border Patrol vehicles streamed onto the north-bound leg, but the other van stayed behind him. It came closer in his mirror as he slowed to pull into the truck-stop, but when Ray turned in, the van continued on.

Ray pumped fuel and casually looked into the truck bed. The old man was sitting up, heaving. His face was pale and his lips were blue. Ray caught the acrid stench of vomit. The other men were squirming under the tarp.

Then Diego sat up. He spoke to the old man, but Ray couldn't hear what he said.

Ray said, "Diego, get him down. The Border Patrol's all around here."

"He is sick," Diego said.

"He'll have to be sick under the tarp."

Diego helped the old guy lie back, then covered him with the stiff canvas. "How much longer to Phoenix?"

"I'll let you know when we get there. Keep those guys down."

When Ray pulled out of the lot, he looked to his left. The Border Patrol van was sitting beside the road. As Ray eased away, the lights of the van came on and it pulled onto the road. When Ray crossed the bridge, there was a line of cars approaching the freeway entrance on his left. If he gunned it he could get on the freeway ahead of the line, and the Border Patrol van behind him would have to wait for the line to clear. He floored the gas pedal. The tires spun on the wet concrete, but the duel wheels caught traction. He swung the wheel to the left and was on the ramp with at least a dozen cars between him and the Border Patrol van.

He took the express lane and floored the gas. He watched his mirror, straining to see if the Border Patrol van was catching up. In the truck bed, two heads poked up. The old man was sitting up again and Diego was trying to get him to lie down. The tarp was billowing and flapping. Ray drifted off the road. He swerved back into his lane, then checked his side mirror. A vehicle was gaining on him fast. When it was nearly on his tail, Ray signaled to change lanes. It was the Border Patrol van, and it changed lanes with him, staying a steady six car-lengths behind.

Ray couldn't keep his eyes away from the mirror. Rain was slamming his windshield, and he was doing 80 on a slick road, but he couldn't keep his gaze from drifting back to that mirror. The green tarp was fluttering in the overdraft. Two heads were visible, then three. The old man was up again, his arms flailing, and two of the others were holding on to him.

The lights of Phoenix were suddenly visible. A sign said it was six miles to the exit Ray wanted. Just six miles, but he knew he'd never make it. The overhead lights flashed on the Border Patrol wagon, the spinning reds and blues sparkling in Ray's mirror.

He was composing his message to Mona when he signaled to pull off. He slowed, and the Border Patrol wagon came right up behind him. As Ray pulled over, the van flashed past him and in a few seconds was lost in the smear of mist and traffic.

Ray stopped the truck. He rolled down the window to get some air, but exhaust fumes drifted into the cab, mingling with the red-onion stench of his sweat. There was an exit just ahead. He stayed in the safety lane all the way and took the exit slowly. At the intersection was a vacant gas station and a cluster of rundown metal buildings, so he pulled under the rusting canopy of the gas station. The rain made a steady drumbeat on the corroded metal roof.

He shut off the engine. He had to get out. His bladder was full, his back was stiff, and his neck muscles were clenched from fear. He stepped down from the truck. The six men were still tucked under the tarp.

"Okay, amigos," he said. "Come on out. It's safe."

The wet canvas heaved and the men uncovered. As they sat up, they looked at the one man who didn't move. Diego pulled the tarp back to look at the old man. Then he covered the man's face. He turned to Ray.

"*Mi amigo viejo, es muerto.*"

Ray couldn't believe it. "He's dead?"

Diego didn't answer. He jumped over the side of the truck. He faced Ray while the other men went off to the side to relieve themselves. "He had a weak heart."

"Why didn't you tell me? Do you think I'd have—" The look on Diego's face shut him up.

Diego took off his hat with his left hand and made the Sign of the Cross with his right. He spoke in a voice so low that Ray could barely hear. "We did not want to bring him with us, but he had not seen his daughter in twenty years. She moved to Phoenix and she never went back to Mexico to see him. He knew he did not have long to live so he asked to come with us. We had to bring him... we had to." Diego laid his right hand on the truck bed and looked at the thin green mound that was the body of Manuel Santa Crux. "Poor old Manny," he said, "He almost made it."

THE STARBOARD BAR

E very man has the same dream. All that varies is the mode of transport.

Dan Foster's vehicle for escaping the shackles of civilization was a 40-foot sloop docked at Mission Bay. Everything he needed, including a supply of old Scotch whisky and some reasonably good champagne, was already aboard, ready to sail for Hawaii and points west. On a blustery weekday morning, shortly before noon, he was hurrying along the chain link fence that bordered the slips, hoping to get underway with the tide. He was carrying a small bag containing charts and personal papers. Aside from his boat and its contents, that bag was all he had in the world. A film of sweat lay between his hand and the grip of that shabby bag and he felt every thumping heartbeat. This was his first solo crossing, in a boat that was new to him, and he feared for his skills. But he'd just turned forty, and it was now or never.

He hopped the five-foot chain link fence and hurried down the wooden dock, but after walking a few feet, he stopped. He dropped his bag, rubbed his tired eyes and stared in disbelief. He knew what he was seeing couldn't be real, so he looked up into the cloud-streaked sky to clear his vision. When he looked again, he had to accept the truth. The slip was empty. His boat had disappeared.

When he got to the empty slip, he looked for broken lines or torn-away cleats. A pink sheet of paper was taped to the chain-link gate. It read *Notice of Maritime Lien* in large black letters. He tried to read the small print, but he had trouble focusing. He did make out the amount: $29,404.00

"They towed it away around eight this morning," someone behind him said. It was Melvin Banks, the fat, bald owner of the boat in the next slip.

Dan reached into his pocket for his cell phone, but remembered that he'd cancelled his service: a cell phone wasn't much use at sea. Then he leaned against the rusty fence and looked down into the Coke-bottle green water of the harbor, trying to make himself believe his boat had vanished just hours before the start of his epic journey.

He felt a bit faint, but when he caught his breath he picked up his bag and walked down the dock. He came to a phone booth, stepped in and called his lawyer. When Ira Meyer answered, Dan didn't bother with formalities. "Ira, what's a Maritime Lien?"

"If you own a boat, it's bad news."

"They towed mine away this morning. I don't even know where it is. I paid cash for that boat. It's mine, free and clear. How can they do this?"

"You have any work done on it you didn't pay for?"

"No."

"Well, I'm not a maritime attorney, but I know these liens don't have to be registered, so sometimes they don't show up when the sale closes… and they never expire."

"But how can they just haul it away with no warning?"

Ira's voice was low and calm, with no hint of sympathy or concern. "You're dealing with a very old law, my friend. It's been around for centuries. Ships docked in ports and hired repairs done, then sailed away without paying. Somewhere in the history of your boat, somebody encumbered it with a lien. Now it's caught up with the boat."

"What can I do to get it back?"

Ira shuffled some papers, then cleared his throat. "Did you buy it from a broker or from the owner?"

"The owner."

There was another pause. Ira liked a moment of silence before he delivered bad news. "You're screwed. Pay the lien, or kiss it goodbye. You might call Harrison and Meade."

"Who's that?"

"Maritime attorneys," Ira said. "Good luck."

The last thing Dan wanted was to talk to another lawyer. He felt a desperate need to smash the phone receiver, but he forced himself to return it gently to the cradle. He stepped out of the booth and looked up and down the docks.

Where could he go now? His house and truck were sold, his only home was his boat, and he had no idea where it was. He picked up his bag and walked along the pier. His feet were numb to the feel of the boards, and he could barely focus his eyes. When he reached the end of the pier, he looked to his left, to the blue horizon. A schooner was raising sail. The white canvas fluttered; then the sails billowed with wind, and the sleek craft heeled to leeward. He watched till it became a dot on the horizon.

When it disappeared, he turned from the sea and went up the steps to the walkway that paralleled the dock. It made no difference which direction he took, so he turned right and shuffled along, holding the rail for support. When he came to the door of the Starboard Bar he felt the need to sit down, so he pushed through the varnished wood doors and stepped inside.

The bar was packed with a noisy lunch crowd, and all the tables were occupied. Dan's knees were so weak he was desperate to get off his feet. When he found a booth occupied by one woman, he asked whether he could join her, motioning toward the crowded barroom.

She looked hesitant, but then nodded.

Dan dropped into the booth and forced himself to smile. The waitress appeared, a tall, thin blonde wearing a ketchup-dappled apron. Dan wanted a shot of whiskey and a beer, and another round to follow, but he said, "Coffee."

He ignored the woman sitting across from him and looked out the window at the vast blue Pacific. Two more boats were leaving the harbor, riding a stiff shore breeze, happily outbound on the ebb.

"Excuse me," the woman said. "Are you all right?"

Dan glanced at her and nodded, but he was so mired in misery that he noticed nothing about her, even her reaction to the blanched, funereal state of his face.

"You look like you've suffered a loss," she said.

He didn't answer. *Just my luck to sit with somebody who wants to talk.*

"I know what it's like to lose something," she said.

Dan had no interest in conversation, but he made a feeble attempt to look interested, so she started a monologue about her recent divorce, her voice mingling with the murmur of the crowd. "It was an awful shock," she said. "My husband didn't even tell me himself. He let the sheriff tell me."

Dan barely heard her, because Ira Meyer's words were echoing repeatedly in his mind. *Pay the lien or kiss it goodbye... pay the lien... pay the lien....*

The woman droned on with her story. "We had no children, so at least nobody was hurt but me. We did have a little boy but... he died." She closed her eyes for a moment. "I know how it feels to lose. You feel so lost, and so angry. You just don't know what to do. And my husband, he had things all planned out, so he pretty much left me with nothing." She looked out the window for a few seconds. "Well... almost nothing."

Dan kept up his weak show of interest, looking at her and nodding once in a while, but he couldn't seem to focus on anything close. He glanced out the window at the glistening sea, aching to be out there, looking back at the shoreline of San Diego, away at last. But he was stuck in a crowded bar, listening to a stranger's woes, with the sorrowful mantra of his lawyer's words recycling in his aching head. He gripped the edges of the table, so angry he wanted to tear it off and throw it through the window, but the woman just went on talking, her voice a little softer.

"He left me for a 24 year old Oriental girl... or I guess I should say a 24 year old Asian woman. I admit, she really is beautiful, but couldn't he at least have told me himself? I wouldn't have blamed him. I can't have children anymore. I think he believes she can give him a son."

Dan was trembling, clenching the tabletop to steady himself. He turned away from the sea and looked at the woman, but at that moment his eyes clouded with rage and he couldn't see her clearly.

She stopped talking. Her face eased into a look of genuine compassion. She reached across the table and squeezed his right hand. "Oh, I'm sorry," she whispered. "I didn't mean to upset you. You've got your own problems, and here I am bothering you with mine. I hope my story hasn't upset you."

Dan managed to calm himself, and when his eyes cleared, he really saw her for the first time. At any other time, he'd be overjoyed to be sitting with such a woman. He guessed she was in her mid-thirties. Her fair skin was unblemished and very lightly tanned. Her dark blue eyes reminded him of deep ocean water, and her long, auburn hair glinted in the afternoon sunlight reflecting off the sea.

"Please excuse me for rambling on," she said, squeezing his hand again. "It's just that... well, you seem so empathetic... so easy to talk to."

He was enjoying the feeling of her hand on his. *What was that she said? Something about losing a child? She lost a child, and then her husband left her? Jesus, what a swine he must have been.*

"Are you a sailor?" she asked.

Squeaking the words through his compressed windpipe, Dan said, "I was."

"I've always wanted to sail. My husband had a boat, but he never—Oh God, I'm sorry. I keep babbling on about myself. Sometimes I can be so thoughtless. Please tell me what's on your mind.

Sometimes it's good to talk about it, even if it hurts. I'll be glad to listen."

Dan couldn't squeeze out a word. What could he say, after hearing a story like hers? He looked out the window again.

She put some money on the table and squirmed out of the booth. Standing beside him, she said, "I'll leave you alone. Again, I'm sorry I upset you. Thanks so much for listening to me."

She walked away. Dan was grateful for the silence. He watched the sea, unable to do anything but let his eyes absorb the light. He knew that if he started thinking, he'd lose his composure and do something stupid, so he just sat. Besides, he had nowhere to go. After a few minutes he felt a faint current of air pass over him, and then a touch on his shoulder. The woman was back, and her clean scent made him forget about the sea.

She sat down across from him, extended her right hand, and pressed his forearm. "Look... I don't know you at all, not even your name, but I have the strangest feeling we have something in common. So I was wondering about something." She paused to look out at the blue water and sky, then turned back to him and quietly said, "I've just come into possession of a very nice sailboat, a 40-foot sloop. It belonged to my husband, and it had some kind of lien against it, but he managed to sell it anyway. My attorney bought the rights to the lien in my name, so

I can keep the boat until the owner pays the lien. Anyway, it was towed from here this morning to a dock just up the road. I'm told there's a big supply of liquor on board, and I was wondering, would you care to join me for a drink?"

A Talk with Fernando Cruz

There are sounds that never fail to grab the attention of the human ear. Nobody ignores the buzz of a rattlesnake, or the anguished cry of a child. But a sound that will bring an instant hush, to a mob near-deaf with rage, is the ratchety snap of the loading action when a twelve-gauge shotgun is pumped.

Ed Drake knew that sound was the last trick he had in his bag. He crouched behind the open door of his patrol car, peeking through its shattered window at an oncoming wall of people. They were citizens of the town of South Tucson, people he had sworn nineteen years ago to serve and protect, and they were bombarding his car with roof tiles and chunks of adobe. His partner, Bailey, was sitting in the front seat, his face streaked with blood, his right hand wrapped in a blood-soaked handkerchief. Three Hispanic males were in the back, arrested for assaulting a police officer.

Drake stood up and raised the shotgun, ready to slide the pump. The crowd's anger echoed through the crumbling adobe walls of the alley. A chunk of concrete sailed toward his head and he ducked, banging his chin of the squad car door. He glanced over at Bailey, whose forehead had been laid open to the bone. Bailey was a rookie, and this was his first day on the job. Drake wondered how an experienced cop like himself could have let a routine day to turn into such a mess....

The afternoon had been quiet, like so many others in the barrio. Drake and Bailey were cruising the streets, watching the normally peaceful citizens go about their business. When they stopped for coffee, Drake told Bailey the only interesting item on their agenda was a talk with a man named Fernando Cruz.

Cruz owned a scrap-metal brokerage, but his real trade was in human beings. He arranged transport of illegals from Mexico to points north and east, his main market being Georgia, where the demand for cheap labor was never satisfied. He had a sideline operation, too: the documentation business. He had contacts at Motor Vehicles and at Social Security. For a grand he could get you a perfect driver's license, and for another fifteen hundred you got a valid Social Secularity number. The sideline paid better than his trade in people, and Cruz had all the customers he wanted.

Ed Drake didn't care much about any of that. As long as Cruz didn't disturb the peace—the peace Drake had sworn to maintain—Drake wouldn't roust him. But the day before, some disturbing infor- mation had come in from back east. It appeared that

Fernando Cruz may have stepped seriously out of bounds, and Drake had to see him about it.

At around three that afternoon, a couple hours before their shift ended, they pulled up at a renovated strip of adobe offices on South Palmas. Bailey was driving. Drake told him to park across the street and said he'd be right back. No sense in the two of them going in. Drake just wanted to ask Cruz a few questions. Cruz had the office on the end of the strip. The door was painted dark green, with a brass plate that read *Southwest Salvage*. Drake opened the door and stepped in.

The room had a high ceiling, polished wood floors, and white walls with no pictures. The only furniture was a black metal desk with a computer on it, and a black leather chair sitting empty behind it. Drake heard a toilet flush. The door to the back room opened and a woman came through. She was Hispanic, young, and a little overweight, and her reaction to the sight of Ed Drake was the same he'd seen a thousand times.

Drake's face had served him well, but it sometimes endangered him. Under his patrol hat was a graying crew cut, but the peak of his hair came down an inch onto his forehead and was visible under the bill of his cap. His wide, jutting brow overhung his deep-set grey eyes. They were small, suspicious eyes, hooded by heavy lids. His nose had been broken beyond repair and was permanently bent to his right. His acne-scarred cheeks were shadowed by prominent cheekbones, and his wide, thin lips gave the impression he was never happy, even when he smiled. The girl recoiled in the same way he'd seen from crooks and the law-abiding alike: nobody believed a man so ugly could be on the right side of the law.

Drake tipped his hat. "*Buenos tardes*. I'm Officer Drake. I'd like to see Señor Cruz. Would you please tell him I'm here?"

"He is no longer here. He has gone home for the day."

Drake nodded, then said, "Can I use the rest-room?" Before the girl could reply, he walked past her into the back office and closed the door.

It was a single room, maybe fifteen by twenty feet. A blackboard stretched along the left wall, marked with schedules and numbers in yellow chalk. A wide mahogany desk occupied the center of the room, the tall chair behind it upholstered in dark grey fabric. A black file cabinet was in one corner, but the rest of the place was bare. Behind the desk was a door. Drake slid back the deadbolt, opened the door, and looked up and down the narrow, walled alley. *Easy place to leave in a hurry.*

He flushed the toilet, then went into the front office, said a polite goodbye to the girl, and stepped out into the glaring Sonoran sunlight. Bailey had the car running and the A/C blowing strong, and a sweep of cold air cooled Drake's sweaty face when he got in. "Fernando's not in," he said. "Turn around and head north."

Cruz had girlfriends, but he was at heart a steady family man. He lived with his wife and two kids in a block of renovated apartments on 30th street. He could afford much better surroundings, but evidently had no interest in advertising the fact. It took five minutes in light traffic to get there.

As they drove down 30th, Drake saw a black late-model Ford pickup parked in front of the apartment. "That's Fernando's truck," he said. "Let's park in the alley. There are times when a cop car's a liability." When they got out, he said, "Let me do the talking."

They went in through the front entrance and up a flight of stairs. The place was newly painted with that beige color that builders use, and the smell of fresh paint hid the usual odors of too many people in too small a space. Drake stopped in front of Apartment 22 and listened. A TV was on inside, the volume very low. He let Bailey stand at the door. If the wife looked through the peephole, he wanted her to see Bailey's smooth schoolboy face and wavy blond hair.

Drake knocked three times. Nothing happened. He knocked again, and a shadow appeared behind the peephole glass. A woman said, in Spanish, "What do you want?"

After 19 years in the barrio, Drake's Spanish was good. He said, "We are police officers. We would like to speak to Señor Fernando Cruz."

Two deadbolts slid and the door eased open. A young woman's face appeared, barely visible in the dim light. "He is not here," she said, looking at Drake as she spoke.

"May we come in, señora?" Drake said.

She slid back the chain and they stepped into the apartment. The heavy red curtains were closed. The only light came from the TV, but she'd muted the sound. The furniture was Mediterranean, covered in black fabric, the tables made of dark wood. The place looked neat and orderly, but the air was heavy and damp.

"I'm Officer Drake, and this is Officer Bailey. We checked at Fernando's office. His assistant said he had gone home. We saw his truck outside. You say he is not here?"

The woman was in the middle of the room, arms folded, looking down at the carpet. She was maybe 18, Drake guessed. He couldn't see her clearly in the half-light, but she looked haggard. Her long black hair covered part of her face. She was wearing a gray T shirt with a red stain down the front, tight, faded jeans, and no makeup.

"When do you expect him?" Drake asked, keeping his voice mild.

The girl shook her head. A baby cried. The sound came from a back bedroom. She turned and left the room. Bailey nudged Drake's arm and pointed to the couch. A little boy, maybe six years old, had just awoken. When he saw the policemen, he screamed, "Mama, dos gringos!"

When the baby in the bedroom quieted, the girl returned and sat on the couch stroking the boy's hair, whispering to him to be quiet. Just as Drake was about to speak, she looked up. "Why do you look for him?"

"I just want to talk with him. When he comes home, tell him Officer Drake wants a word with him. He knows who I am."

The boy was looking at them, his lower lip sticking out and his fists doubled.

"I will not tell him," the girl said. "I do not have to tell him. Now get out of our apartment."

Drake didn't understand the reason for her attitude, but he didn't want to make anything of it. The baby cried again, and she left the couch to go to it. The little boy didn't like being abandoned. He started to get up to go after her, but she spun around and told him to get back on the couch. Drake knew it was time to get out of there, but he wanted a couple more words with the girl.

She came back to the living room, holding the baby. Her grey sweatshirt had a dark stain on the shoulder where the baby had soaked it.

"You come here and wake them both up," she said. "Please go away."

Drake eased back toward the door. Then the baby let out a shriek. Drake knew the girl was scared and the baby was sensing her fear. He was about to apologize when the little boy got off the couch. He trotted over and stood in front of his mom. "Leave my mama alone!" he said, this time in good English.

"Sorry about waking the kids," Drake said. "Please tell Fernando I want to see him. He knows how to reach me."

The baby was screaming louder.

"I tell him nothing! Get the hell out!"

Drake had started to reach for the doorknob when the little boy ran toward Bailey. He swung his fist overhand and caught Bailey in the crotch. The hit was so direct and solid that Drake felt it in his own gut.

Bailey bent forward and let out a hoarse grunt.

Then the kid kicked him, hard. He was wearing pointy-toed cowboy boots, but the kick was just an insult. He tried to kick again and Bailey grabbed him. The boy sank his teeth into the meaty part of Bailey's right hand just above the little finger, and he wouldn't let go. He held on like a pit bull, shaking his head from side to side.

The baby let out another scream, her tiny round face hooded by the white blanket, her little arms wiggling.

Then somebody knocked on the door.

Bailey had grabbed the boy's head, trying to break his clench. The boy was punching, and when Bailey went down on one knee, he caught a fist in his left eye.

Drake bent to grab the kid.

The mother screamed, "Leave my boy alone! Leave him alone! Get out!"

The knocking at the door changed to pounding. A man shouted from the hallway, "Juanita, what's going on in there?" Drake moved to the door and eased both deadbolts shut, then went to help Bailey. He tried to squeeze the sides of the kid's jaw, but the boy held on, still punching. The kid opened his hands and started clawing at Bailey's face. Bailey tried to straighten up, but he was still feeling the blow to his crotch. The kid shook his head again, then pulled away, a chunk of Baileys hand in his mouth.

Bailey screamed in pain. "You little bastard!" he said, staring at the half-moon of flesh missing from the side of his hand. The boy spit out the bloody flesh and spat again to clear his mouth. Blood and spit dribbled from his lips. He clenched a fist. "Leave my mama and sister alone or I *kill* you, gringo!"

Drake took Bailey by the arm and backed toward the door. He looked through the peephole. There were faces, but couldn't tell how many. He hollered through the door, "We are police officers. Back away. We are coming out."

Bailey was holding his right hand and wrapping it in a handkerchief. His face was scratched and his left eye was bloodshot. Drake had no idea what would happen in the hallway. It was time to radio for help.

The baby was still crying. The girl was trying to hold back the boy, but he kept shouting curses. "*Puercos! Puercos feo!* Pigs! Ugly pigs!"

Drake looked again through the peephole. Whoever was standing there must have been a big man because all Drake saw was his chest.

Somebody in the hall said, "Open up."

Bailey had his hand wrapped up good, but the girl was about to lose her grip on the boy. The noise behind the door had the kid even more scared.

Drake pulled his radio from his belt. He pushed the call button, but the instant he started to talk, the door came at him. It blew away from the wall, bringing the jamb with it, hitting him broadside. He fell sideways and went down. On top of him was a metal entry door and three Hispanic guys—one very large and two average size—and three more rushing in behind.

Bailey stepped sideways to get in front of the woman and baby. The boy must have thought he was going for his mom, and he shook loose from her and grabbed Bailey around the leg. He bit Bailey on the thigh, but Bailey ignored him.

The three guys on the door struggled to get up.

Drake looked stunned, but he was moving.

Bailey was trying to get to him, but one of the guys, the biggest one, reached for Bailey and grabbed his shirt. Bailey wrenched to the side, pulled his stick, swung around to his right with the boy still biting his thigh, and caught the big man across the face.

The blow stunned the guy, but another man came at Bailey. Bailey must have known he couldn't fend off more than one guy with his stick. He had only one choice: he had to get everyone's attention. He pulled his pistol from his belt and aimed at the big man, who had staggered back and was bleeding from the blow to his face. In a calm, steady voice, he said, "Stand back."

The mother stopped screaming. Bailey grabbed the boy by the back of his neck and squeezed. The kid let go.

Drake was getting to his feet.

"You all right?" Bailey asked.

Drake straightened up slowly, his hand on his back. He had no visible signs of damage, but his hat had come off and his face had gone pale. He looked for his radio and found it on the floor near the kitchen door. He pushed the buttons, but nothing happened.

Bailey turned to the woman as everyone in the room watched him. "Where's the phone?"

She shook her head.

"The phone, please." Bailey's voice was quiet, with no sign of panic in it.

She shook her head again.

Drake's first instinct was to take over the situation, but the rookie with his gun drawn had everybody's attention. Drake stepped over the door, careful not to get too close to the big Hispanic guy. Bailey had the gun aimed at that guy and the two standing beside him. Three others were standing aside in a cluster, hands raised, with scared, angry looks on their dark faces. The doorway was crowded, and Drake still couldn't tell how many were in the hall. At this point, all he wanted was for him and Bailey to escape. Maintaining respect for the law was no longer an issue.

But Bailey saw it different. "You're under arrest," he said to the three guys who'd crashed the door, "for assaulting a police officer."

One of the three, wearing a red T shirt and jeans, stepped forward with his hands up. He spoke in broken English. "We thought somebody was messing with the woman and her kids. We don't see no cop car. We think bad things happen. We not know you are cops... police."

Bailey said, "Back up against the wall."

There was nothing Drake could do now. He didn't want to leave towing three men under arrest, but Bailey had dealt the hand and Drake had to play it out with him. They got the three guys cuffed, and Drake spoke quietly to the girl. "I am sorry for this mess. We'll be going now. But tell Fernando I need to talk to him." Drake turned to go. The boy hissed something in Spanish that Drake couldn't translate.

Bailey had the three guys lined up, ready to go downstairs. The crowd jamming the doorway backed up. "All right, move forward, out the door and down the back stairs." Bailey said. He had his pistol pointed at the big guy's back.

The crowd parted as they passed through the hallway. They were mostly working men, just home from their jobs, their T-shirts dirty and sweaty, but they had that stone-faced look that Hispanic guys get when they're about to go over the edge. Despite his fear, Drake felt sympathy for them. These were law-abiding people, but they believed their home had been invaded. He looked straight ahead as he led the parade, avoiding eye contact and praying that nobody made a threatening move.

They got through the crowd and down the back stairs, then headed out to the alley. There were more people in the alley, and they had already made their feelings known, having smashed the front and side windows of the patrol car.

Bailey squeezed the three Hispanics into the back seat and locked the back doors. Drake slid into the driver's seat after brushing away the bits of glass. His first thought was to radio for help, but the dash had been ripped up. He put the key in and turned it. The engine started. He shouted to Bailey to get in, and when Bailey opened the door, something hit him in the forehead. It was a piece of terra cotta roof tile, spun like a Frisbee. It struck him at his hairline and knocked him back. He stumbled and fell against the broken adobe wall of the alley.

Drake was about to get out to help, but Bailey got to his feet. He stumbled to the car, slid onto the seat and pulled the door shut. Something hit what remained of the windshield, and small squares of glass sprinkled into their laps. Drake slid the gearshift down.

But the alley was blocked, and the crowd was moving forward. Most of them were young, wearing ball caps or bandanas, and they were heaving things at the car. Drake turned to the rear. A smaller crowd, moving just as fast, was coming on from behind. He looked at the broken dashboard, then at his bleeding partner. He had to get control of this situation, and he had only one option left.

He unlocked the shackle that held the twelve-gauge pump, took the gun from the metal bracket, and eased the door open. He slid out of the seat and stood up behind the door. He dodged a chunk of concrete aimed at his head, then raised the shotgun, slid the action back to load the chamber, and aimed the fat black barrel at the pressing crowd.

Everybody stopped. A clod of mud adobe hit the roof of the car and scattered in dry bits across the alley, but no more projectiles flew. The only noise came from traffic out on Stone Avenue. Drake had their attention, but he was at a loss for what to do now. He was holding back the mob with the gun, but he was not going to shoot into a crowd of unarmed men.

He looked at the men in front of the crowd. He had thought his shotgun had their attention, but they weren't looking at him. Drake glanced to his left. Standing three feet from him, dressed in a starched white dress shirt and blue jeans, was Fernando Cruz.

The alley was so quiet the rustle of his boots on the gravel made the only sound. Cruz took two steps and stopped inches from the battered car door. "Officer Drake," he said. "I am told you wish to speak to me."

Drake raised the gun barrel, pointing it at the sky. He straightened up and looked at Cruz.

The two men had spoken only twice, but Drake's impression of Cruz hadn't changed. They were the same height, but Cruz was a little heavier. His smooth, round face was the color of bronze, and his wavy black hair was neatly combed, but there was some gringo blood in him, because his eyes were pale blue. His full lips were always upturned in a benevolent smile. Drake wondered how this must look like to the crowd, a cop with a mobster face confronting a choir-boy crook.

Cruz was waiting for Drake to make his move, and so was the crowd. Drake just wanted to get himself and his partner out of that alley.

"Hello Fernando," he said. "Glad to see you."

Cruz raised his hands, palms upward. "I come home, my front door is lying on my living room floor. My wife and children are upset. Why are you doing this to me?"

Drake looked at the crowd, then back at Cruz. "It was all a big misunderstanding."

"Sure. That's what we say to you cops all the time, but you never seem to believe us. It was all a big misunderstanding?"

Drake was not going to justify himself, but he had to get out of that alley, and he needed Cruz to help him. Cruz knew that as well as Drake did. Here was a chance to put two gringo cops in his debt. He raised his hands to the crowd and spoke in Spanish. "Amigos. My wife and children are unharmed. These men who are under arrest are my good friends. I assure you they will be treated fairly by the police. Would you please stand back and let them pass?"

Nobody moved.

Cruz raised his arms to both crowds, motioning for them to move back. Then he stepped away from the car.

Drake laid his arm on the car door, trying to look casual. He spoke as quietly as he could to Cruz, not wanting to be overheard. "I appreciate your help, Fernando, but I will be back."

"You want to come back and make more trouble in our peaceful neighborhood?"

"You and me still have to talk."

"What about? You know I am a legitimate business man."

Drake was getting impatient. The fear and loss of control were wearing on him. "We need to talk about a man named Haziz Mohammed," Drake said. He studied Fernando's face. Not a twitch or a flicker showed.

"Don't know him," Cruz said.

"He's a Middle-Eastern chap. He told the FBI he got his documentation in Tucson, Arizona, from a Hispanic fellow, one with blue eyes... but like I said, we'll talk another time."

Drake slid behind the wheel and laid the shotgun on the floor. When he slammed the door a shower of glass bits fell into his lap. He slipped the gearshift lever into Drive and moved at a crawl out of the alley, peering through the football-shaped hole in the shattered windshield. The crowd edged to the side, leaving just enough room for the car to pass.

Drake stopped at the end of the alley. He took off his hat, wiped his face on his shirtsleeve, and looked at his partner. "Well, Officer Bailey, how do you like police work?"

Bailey lowered his bloodstained hand. "I like it fine."

Drake believed him. But he knew if the same thing had happened nineteen years ago, on *his* first day on the job, he'd be celebrating his twentieth year in another line of work.

The Dark Side of Enlightenment

I hadn't seen John Gurney in over thirty years. Truth is, the last time I saw him I was trying to run over him with my '69 Chevy. I'd made a serious attempt to kill the man back then, and as I stood at a pay phone in downtown Missoula, dialing a number I hoped was his, I wondered how he'd come to terms with that ugly incident from our past.

After six rings, he answered. I knew it was him, but I asked anyway.

"This John Gurney?"

"Who's asking?

"Rick Campbell. You remember me?"

After a long pause, he said, "Yeah. Where are you?"

"Downtown."

"What're you doing up here in Montana?"

"Out for a drive, thought I'd stop in."

"Out for a drive? I heard you were in prison down in Arizona."

I hesitated, then said, "I was. In Florence. I'm on parole."

"Well, what'd you call me for?"

"Chat maybe? Old time sake?"

He gave me directions to a tavern called the Oxford, just a block away. I found it, went in and sat at the bar, and I was on my second beer when Gurney walked in. He looked the same, just older, but his bowlegged gait had a bad limp I'd never seen. He stuck out a hard, dry hand and I shook it.

I was sure he'd bring up the nasty episode from our past, but he launched into a series of stories about his adventures in Montana, where he'd moved right after the last time I saw him. After our fifth beer, I thought he might be loose enough to talk about my attempt to run him over, and when I asked whether he remembered it, he took a sip of beer and said, "We'll talk about that tomorrow." I wanted to settle the issue there and then, but I said okay. He gave me the name of a fleabag motel and offered to buy me breakfast in the morning.

It was a good breakfast and it was dirt cheap, and when we finished it, I thought it was time I got to my purpose. After the waitress poured coffee, I said, "I guess you're wondering why I'm here after all this time."

"You said you was out for a drive."

"I wanted to talk about that time I tried to run you over. I mean, I really was trying to kill you. I wondered at times how you felt about that. Anyway, I came up here to—"

"Talk about that later. Ever been up to Glacier National Park? Weather's not too bad. Be a shame to come all this way and not see it."

I wanted to stick to my subject, but he stood up and paid the bill. "I'll drive," he said.

We went outside to his rusty Cherokee. I shoved a bunch of trash out of the passenger seat, and when I shut the door, I sneezed from the dust. He drove west on I-90 and then turned north. Along the way, he had a story for every bend in the road.

"See that dirt road? Monty and me went down there once and damn near ran into a moose. It was standing right in the middle of the road. All we had with us was a .22. Monty put fifteen rounds into that big bull, but he kept on running. We found it about a mile over that ridge, lying in a patch of weeds, still kicking. Monty finished it with a big rock, said he'd wasted enough ammunition on it."

The stories continued for about a hundred miles. His tales got irritating after a while, but the truth was, I was envious: while I'd been pissing my life away as a crook, Gurney was up here in nature-land, having a hell of a good time.

We stopped for a greasy lunch, and when we were on a stretch of empty road, I decided to speak my mind. "I came up here to talk to you about what I did back there in the alley behind Myers's place, trying to run you over. I wanted to ask you if you'd—"

"I told you, man, we'll talk about it later."

"Fuck later. I drove a long way for this. Now listen to me."

He swerved onto a muddy side road so fast that I almost spilled into his lap. As soon as he got control he looked at me and said, "Ever been in woods this deep?"

It was like we were in a tunnel. The shaggy pines were packed close together, black and mossy and dripping with melting snow. You couldn't see three feet into them. Gurney slowed for a boggy area, then shifted into four-wheel drive. He floored the gas and we muddled through.

"Up ahead about a mile's the prettiest little trout stream you ever saw."

"John, I don't want to see a trout stream. I came up here to ask you to forgive me for what I did."

I waited for an answer but he just kept on driving. The road dwindled to a pair of ruts and then was blocked by a dead tree. He stopped and shut off the motor. "Let's go for a walk." He went around the back and pulled out a holstered handgun and a pump shotgun. When he saw my raised eyebrows, he said, "Bears are getting up. They'll be hungry."

I said, "Look man, I don't want to walk. I came up here to ask your forgiveness for what I did. I'm sorry and I wish I had some way to make amends, but I can't think of any."

"What the fuck's with you? You get religion or something?"

"I got with this Buddhism thing," I said. "They call it enlightenment. I learned that we cause our own suffering. I learned to let go of attachments and grudges and blame. All I want now's forgiveness from anybody I hurt. That's why I'm here." I told him more about how I'd changed in prison, hoping to say it in a way he'd understand, but all I got was a blank stare.

Then Gurney handed me the shotgun. "Let's walk. You go first."

He strapped on his sidearm and pointed to a faint trail. I didn't want to argue, so I started walking. It was mostly slush and mud. I had to bend over to get under branches, and I felt queasy with him behind me, but I knew the shotgun was loaded. Problem was, the brush was so thick I'd never turn around in time, not with this unwieldy gun.

The trail ended at a creek. It was just like he'd said, pretty as a picture and gurgling with snowmelt. When I turned around, he had that gun in his hand, aimed at me. "So you came here to ask forgiveness for crippling me?"

I looked at that gun. It had a bore the size of a dime. "What do you mean, crippled? You got out of the way."

"Yeah, and I trashed my knee in the process. Where you think I got this limp?"

"Okay, I admit, it was stupid trying to kill you over a girl."

"A girl? What the fuck you talking about?"

"I heard you were messing around with Dixie."

"That's why you tried to run me over?"

"Hell yes. Why'd you think?"

Gurney laughed. "I thought you'd found out it was me who framed you for stealing from the store."

The rustle of that creek was the only sound. I thought back to that day back in 1980, when I was accused of a series of thefts from a store where Gurney and I worked. I was innocent, but I was sentenced to two years in prison. I never got over the injustice of it, and for almost thirty years afterward, I was a vicious criminal. And the man who set me on that path was standing in front of me. "That was you?"

"Yeah. I figured that's why you tried to run me over, not for some silly shit about Dixie. You're so big on forgiveness, you gonna forgive *me*?" He laughed, the gun drooping at his side

I reminded myself what the Buddha had said about the causes of our problems, and that we should face all things with equanimity. I conjured Jesus, and I heard him tell me to forgive. Then my mind cleared and I knew what I had to do.

Some say enlightenment's a gradual thing. Some say it comes all at once. When I raised that shotgun and aimed it a Gurney's gut, I saw in a flash just how enlightened I really was.

⟶⟶ ⟶⟶ ⟶⟶ ⟶⟶ ⟶⟶

A Voyage to Pluto

On a sunny morning in January, shortly before noon, a hard-packed snowball left the meaty hand of Mike Stowe and sailed in a low arc over the crowded playground of St. Martin's School. It was a retaliatory strike aimed at Eddie O'Neal, and when Eddie saw it coming, he ducked behind the only cover available: the short, squat body of Sister Marie David.

The snowball exploded against the back of her head, sending a shower of crystals into the crisp winter air. The impact jarred her glasses to the end of her nose, but her center of gravity was so low that she stumbled, but didn't fall. When she looked down she saw Eddie crouching. Their eyes met. Eddie didn't move.

She spun around to find the thrower, but Stowe had vanished in the swirling mob. She turned back to Eddie, who hadn't budged. She bent down and seized his left ear, giving it a hard twist as she pulled him upright. She lowered her face. Her stale breath assaulted Eddie's nose. "Who did it?"

Eddie looked up at the round moon of her face. It was framed by the starched white linen of her habit, and her rimless glasses magnified her pale gray eyes. He was helpless and too terrified to speak.

"Who did it?"

Eddie remained silent.

"Come with me, Mr. O'Neal."

She pulled him toward the school building. As they approached the steps, Eddie looked up and saw Deana James staring at him. Deana was the prettiest girl in the eighth grade, and Eddie worshipped her. Her sneer of disgust distracted him and he tripped on the stairs, but Sister Marie held him up by his twisted ear.

They pushed through the green metal doors and marched down the deserted hall. Eddie's head was cranked sideways, and all he could see was the shiny terrazzo floor streaking by. When they reached Sister Marie's office, she plopped him down in the dark oak chair in front of her desk, then let go of Eddie's ear. He put his hand to it to ease the throbbing.

Sister Marie stood over him, swaying slightly forward and back, her sways in harmony with the steady ticking of the wall clock. The weight of her gaze bore down on the back of his neck. "Look at me, Mr. O'Neal."

Eddie couldn't.

"Look at me!"

He was crouched forward, his hands on his knees. He raised his head and looked into the lunar face hovering above.

"Tell me who did it."

He held her gaze as long as he could, then looked away.

"Look at me!"

Fearing the consequence, he looked up again. He focused on the pockmarked skin of her pale, rounded cheeks.

"If you don't tell me, I will expel you from this school. You will walk out that door and never come back."

The wall clock ticked. Louder, it seemed. Eddie was trembling. He dug his fingernails into his bony knees, trying to steady himself. Expelled! That would be worse than death. He would disgrace his entire family. All his brothers and sisters went to St. Martin's. They'd have to bear his shame.

But he couldn't tell on Stowe. Stowe was his best friend. They were co-captains on the football team and Eddie helped Stowe with his homework because Stowe wasn't good at school but was good at everything else and Stowe didn't have a dad and his mom was always having nervous breakdowns and if Eddie ratted Stowe out, Stowe would get expelled too and he wouldn't get to go to Central Catholic High School and that was his only chance to get a football scholarship and maybe go to college. Eddie was sure that if he gave in to Sister Marie, Stowe's future would be ruined.

"Look at me!" she said again.

He forced himself to look up.

Sister Marie loomed, her face a radiant white, waiting. "This is your last chance. Who did it?"

A thought ripped through Eddie's mind, a vision of how his dad would look at him when he heard the news of the expulsion. It was more than Eddie could bear. He let go of his knees and clamped his hands over his ears. He didn't want to hear himself say the word. *Please don't say it,* he begged. *Please don't.* In a hoarse, dry whisper, he said, "Stowe."

Sister Marie heard the name, but she made him repeat it. "What did you say?"

Eddie tried to say it louder, but his lungs felt empty. He squeezed the name out with his last bit of breath. "Stowe."

When the word passed his lips, he slumped. He wrapped his arms around himself, trying to stay in the chair.

Sister Marie let out a long sigh. Eddie shivered as her breath flowed over him.

"You may go home for lunch now, Mr. O'Neal."

Eddie couldn't move. Sister Marie left the office. He sat, listening to the echo of her heels on the hard, polished floor. His eyes puddled. He looked at the floor and watched the drops splatter at his feet.

He got up and walked home with his eyes downcast, across the snow-packed schoolyard, down South Street and one block over to Cambridge, the street he lived on. The front of his jacket was damp in places with the tears that fell steadily off his cheeks.

He paused at the door of his house and looked at the brass doorknob. Then he turned the knob and went in. His younger brothers and sisters were arguing in the kitchen. He passed through the dining room and was met by his mother at the kitchen door

"Where have you been?" she said. She looked closely at his face." Did you have another fight with the Ramsey brothers?"

He looked into his mother's large brown eyes. He glanced at the bright green cloth she'd tied in her hair. Her arms were folded in front of her. He took a step back, to be out of reach of her swing. "Stowe threw a snowball at me. It hit Sister Marie. She made me tell her who did it."

The noise in the kitchen stopped. His siblings were listening. His mother let her hands drop to her side. "You mean you told on your best friend? You told on Mike Stowe?"

Eddie's couldn't digest the words. All his life, he'd been taught that nuns were the handmaidens of God and to defy them was a moral outrage. Sassing a nun was like giving God the finger. "But Mom, she said she'd kick me out. She said she'd kick me out of school."

"I don't care what she said. Mike Stowe is your best friend. Now it's him who'll get kicked out of school. How does that make you feel?"

He felt stricken. Nothing could sting him more than his mother's angry words. Another chill waved through him. He couldn't seem to get any air in his lungs.

"Eat your lunch and wash your face," she said. "You haven't got much time."

His throat was too tight to swallow food, so he went to the bathroom and surveyed his face. He could wash away the streaks, but he would have to go back to school red-eyed.

Later, in the schoolyard, it took him several minutes to find Mike Stowe, who was talking to Cathy Bishop. Stowe could have any girl in the 8th grade class, but plain and chubby Cathy Bishop was the only girl he liked. When Eddie walked up to them, Stowe looked at Eddie's red eyes. "What's wrong, Eddie?"

Eddie grabbed the sleeve of Stowe's jacket and pulled him away from Cathy. He turned to face his friend, raising his chin to make it an easy target. He looked straight into Stowe's cold blue eyes. "I told, Mike. Sister Marie knows it was you."

Stowe looked away, toward the tall chimney that rose over the parking lot. A slight smile raised the corners of his thin lips. Mike Stowe knew nothing of the concept of fatalism, but he'd learned early in his life never to expect much from anyone, least of all loyalty. He nodded, put his oversized hand on Eddie's shoulder and squeezed, then let his hand fall to his side. "Don't worry, Eddie. It's no big deal."

Stowe turned and walked back to Cathy Bishop. Eddie stood still for a moment, wishing with all his heart that Stowe had hit him.

They filed back into class. When they were all seated, Sister Rosario closed the shiny oak door and began the afternoon lessons. Eddie watched the door, knowing that at any moment it would open and Sister Marie would come in. She would stand near Mike Stowe and point to the door. Stowe would rise, look down at Eddie, and walk out. Eddie played the frightful scene over and over in his mind.

The lessons ground on. First came math and then history, and then science. The science lesson was about astronomy. Sister Rosario talked about Pluto, which was the farthest planet from the sun. She said that some people didn't think Pluto was really a planet anymore, but Sister Rosario was from New Mexico, and in New Mexico, she said, they still say it's a planet. Then she said it took Pluto almost 250 years to make a single orbit. Eddie felt a cold sting in his heart when he heard that. He'd listened closely to the lesson, but he couldn't keep his eyes off the door.

They hurried through the art lesson, and still the door remained closed. Sister Rosario dinged the little bell on her desk, and the class rose for the final prayer. Eddie glanced at Stowe, who was chewing gum and looking out the window.

The exit from school was routine, and Eddie hurried home. He went to his room and sat on the floor near his bed. He put on his blue wool stocking cap and pulled it down over his eyes, waiting for his dad to come home.

When the afternoon grew dark, he heard his dad's voice downstairs. Then his mother called him to dinner. Dinner went as usual. Eddie looked at his father, but his father didn't look back. After dinner he treaded up the steps, did his homework, and waited for his dad to call him downstairs. Then, it was 9 o'clock and time to go to bed. Eddie's father came up to use the bathroom, and as Eddie lay in bed, he heard his father's footsteps in the hallway. Those footsteps paused at the door of the bedroom Eddie shared with his two younger brothers, but then his father slowly descended the stairs.

Eddie couldn't sleep, so he slid out of bed and sat on the floor, looking out the window. The bitter winter air was clear. Clusters of stars sprinkled the moonless night.

He had no way of knowing that at that moment, Sister Marie was on her knees in the convent chapel, praying for the soul of her dying father. He couldn't know that Mike Stowe was mopping vomit from the kitchen floor because his mother had come home drunk. He couldn't know that downstairs his parents were huddled at the kitchen table, trying to figure a way to make the next house payment. All he knew was that somewhere in that black, indifferent space above him, tiny Pluto was making its lonely journey, cold, dark, and so very far from the sun.

About the Author

Bruce Weber lives in Tucson, where he is self-employed. His first novel, *Dark Manna*, was released in 2012. The writer who has influenced him most is James M. Cain, who wrote *Double Indemnity*, *Mildred Pierce*, and *The Postman Always Rings Twice*. Bruce Weber's next novel, *Prayers For The Devil* will be out later in 2015.

CPSIA information can be obtained
at www.ICGtesting.com
Printed in the USA
LVHW081416091019
633565LV00033B/937/P

9 781508 517832